MW01077173

★★★★★★★★★★★★★★★★★★★★★★★★★

THE LAST

ROCK AND ROLL SHOW

★★★★★★★★★★★★★★★★★★★★★★★★★

www.thelastrockandrollshow.com
www.myspace.com/thelastrockandrollshow
www.16ton.com

Edited by: Jerri Bergen and Kathleen Kramer
Book Layout: Kay Meadows
Cover Design: Rick von Dehl
www.airshowcreative.com

For Dad
so we could spend some
time together again

ACKNOWLEGEMENTS

The Last Rock and Roll Show would not have been possible without the support from some very special people, and the good Lord above. First, I must thank my family. Their love and energy encouraged me to finish this book. To Mom; a 1959 high school graduate who helped me with the history I couldn't figure out on my own. Endless thanks to Tommy Allsup, a great pal, who along with the memory of my Dad was the inspiration for this book. To my readers: Holly White, Alec Pappas, Robert Reynolds, Bob Saporiti, Mike Crouch, and Tony ""Chico" Smith. To Martin Lynds for copy editing. Special thanks to Kay Meadows for the book layout. To Kevin Montgomery and all my musician pals that cheered me on. Special recognition goes to Rick von Dehl for his fabulous artwork and attention to detail, which resulted in the ultimate, classic book cover. A special thanks to my editors, Jerri Bergen and Kathleen Kramer for their cheerful energy, enthusiasm, and honesty. I couldn't have hoped to find a better editing team for this first novel. Finally, I want to thank the Buddy Holly, Ritchie Valens, and Big Bopper fans of England and Scotland. You're love of their music compelled me to put pen, to paper.

PROLOGUE
CLEAR LAKE, IOWA FEBRUARY 2, 1959

Michael always loved the movies as a child, pretending to be his silver screen heroes, constantly re-enacting scenes from movies that his mother would take him to see. One such movie was James Dean's *Rebel Without A Cause*. Dean's second film, that some say was the most powerful performance of the actor's short career, stunned the young man.

When Michael walked out of the theater that October day in 1955, he knew what he was destined to do. He imagined his own mental image in the likeness of Dean, with his careless arrogance, and burning passions. Dean lived life at the speed of sound, or at least that's the way it appeared on the big screen to Michael. He wanted to live life the same way. He was impressed by the star's ability to rise from small town obscurity to the heights of film industry greatness. If James Dean from Fairmont, Indiana, could do it, then Michael Minton from Clear Lake, Iowa, could do it too.

Michael's excitement and love for the big screen however, faded less than two years later when his mother died in a car accident near Des Moines. Devastated, he lost much of his motivation to pursue his dream, running on autopilot, seeing no further than the daily toil with his tow truck while drifting into obscurity.

The thought of leaving his Dad to run the family business alone entered his thoughts, but only briefly. Each time he guiltily squashed the impulse, reminding himself of the additional burden his father would be left to bear, resigning himself to a role that the unfortunate circumstances of life had cast him in. All the shining points of light that were once so bright were gone, his life nothing more than a dim spec of stardust on a far off horizon.

Michael found himself pondering as he drove through the dark. The snow tires of the big International bit through the drifts, and crunched through the ice. He whispered to himself . . .

What could I have accomplished in life? If only things were different?

After arriving back at the shop, Michael parked wrecker #3 in the expansive corrugated metal garage that belonged to his Dad. He was glad to be back in front of the ancient, wood burning parlor stove to thaw his frozen bones. His Dad's torn and frayed desk chair looked like hell, but felt like heaven as he stretched out his legs and drifted off to sleep.

Just after he dozed off, Eddie arrived back at the shop and kicked the chair underneath Michael, waking him up.

"Kid." He bellowed. "I'm going home and you should to. Lock it up."

The steel gray door slammed shut behind Eddie with a bang, knocking the Polly Gas clock above the desk to the floor. It was 1:07a.m. A snow spray caught in the updraft of the closing door, dropped unceremoniously all over the back of Michael's neck, and down his back.

Just then, and in a split second, something happened. The relative calm Michael briefly enjoyed after the long work night, nourished by the warmth of the stove, turned into a cold, and desperate rage.

Maybe it was his mother's death, or the feeling that she was cheated out of her young life that sparked the madness. Or maybe, it was the certainty he felt that his mother's life, was a life that ended unfulfilled. Two years of suppressed resentment that was boiling just under his skin, came crashing to the surface, obliterating the façade he was living behind. He was pretending to be happy. He was far from it.

Selfishly, he didn't want the same, miserable fate that his mother suffered for himself. Clear Lake couldn't offer him the opportunity that his hurting soul longed for. He could do better. He would do better. The time had come.

He leapt out of the creaky shop chair and whirled around to the company money drawer, stuffing bills deep into the pocket's of his blue jeans. Quiet desperation gripped him as he put the gold watch his granddad gave him for his sixteenth birthday on the desk along with his shop keys. He scribbled a short note for his Dad, and tucked it under the dial of the telephone.

I'm sorry. I'll make the money up to you in the next couple of months. I need to leave now before it's too late. I love you. Goodbye.

Michael slowed, awash with emotion as tears began to form at the corners of his eyes. Then, he gathered himself with steely resolve, re-focusing on his new found vision for an escape from a life he had grown to hate. He reached under the desk, pulled open the bottom drawer, then retrieved a small set of tools he used for picking door locks.

Opening the door of the nearest car he could find was easy. He was trained to do just that for scores of sorry motorists who locked their keys in their cars, lost them in the lake, or hiking in the woods, or one of a hundred other reasons. Putting the car in reverse, he rolled out of the shop and into the parking lot. Then, without looking back, he drove away into the cold and deadly Iowa night.

★★★★★★★★★★★★★★★★★★★★★★★★★★★★

FEBRUARY 2, 1959
THE WINTER DANCE PARTY

★★★★★★★★★★★★★★★★★★★★★★★★★★★★

1

7:30 P.M., CLEAR LAKE, IOWA

"You drove the Cadillac?" DJ Evans uttered in disbelief, amazed at his best friends questionable judgment.

"Yeah, so what?" Billy answered. "Jump in and get out of the cold already."

"So what? There's a full scale blizzard rolling in. You know you're out of your mind, right? Not only that, but you're going to be in Dutch up to your neck if he finds out." DJ pulled his letterman's jacket up over his neck in an attempt to block the pellets of gritty snow whipping down the sidewalk in the ferocious wind.

"Ease up, Chief." Billy said calmly. "I'm just borrowing it for a few hours."

On the sidewalk, their dates huddled close together, shivering as the boys talked about the car. A little embarrassed and fearful they might turn from ravishing beauties into gorgeous ice statues, the friends turned and helped the girls toward the car. The movements of their pointy-tip stilettos cracked pea size holes in the ice as they got into the dazzling green Cadillac Eldorado Brougham.

"OK. I got the part about borrowed, since we all know this isn't your ride." DJ eyed the car as he got into the passenger side of the pristine caddy, "that much I've got."

Billy Daniels knew the berating was coming. The two had been best friends for as long as he could remember, and they always looked out for each other. However, at the moment it was a painful annoyance with the girls in the car.

DJ continued the lashing. "But what I don't get is the kind of nose-bleed you are that thinks you can take your Uncle's brand new Cadillac out and not get a scratch, dent, or water spot on it on one of the worst nights of the winter!"

"Look DJ, it's just for tonight." Billy said shortly, giving him one last silencing stare. "I'll clean it up in the morning, put it back in the garage, and no one will ever know the difference. Besides, the girls like it, right ladies?"

"We do, Billy." They cooed in concert, giggling at the identical timing of their answer.

Barbara and Bobbie Lynn Compton were Mason City's knock-out identical twins and every guy's fantasy date in the county. Since the twins were courted by many suitors, the girls were accustomed to the finer things, and could afford to be choosy in regard to who they dated. Which guy had the fastest car? Who would take them to the finest restaurant? Who would lavish them with flowers and all the rest?

On the surface, the Compton twins seemed sweet, coy and well-mannered. However, they used their intoxicating beauty, charm, and feigned innocence to manipulate many a guy in the area. The

Compton's considered free tickets to the show, and a ride in the new Cadillac, a "dreamy" set up.

"No big deal Billy." DJ conceded, ignoring his friend's lack of apparent concern. "It's no sweat off my back. But don't be surprised if ole' Earl notices the extra few miles on the odometer when he gets back home."

"Everything's going to be perfect DJ. Trust me."

Turning the car full of excited rock 'n' roll fans onto West Division Avenue, the ice laden street crunched and moaned under the tires of the super heavy weight luxury car. Navigating the treacherous side streets gingerly, Billy rolled to a smooth stop at 460 North Shore Drive. Low fog drifting in from the lake across the street hung heavy around the flashing indigo marquee of The Surf Ballroom, glowing in the Cadillac's meticulous paint.

Barb Compton, tired of the exchange between the boys, momentarily allowed her sapphire blues eyes to stray from the mirror in her compact. She drew a large sigh of relief when they arrived

"I need to be close to the stage," she moaned, batting her long black eyelashes at DJ. "I just love dancing to Ritchie's songs. I want to *feel* the music. Can you do that for me, lover?"

Barb's voice filled with a female urgency that DJ recognized as a "need to do" versus "nice to do" request.

"Can I do that?" He replied, as if it were a forgone conclusion. "Just stick with me little lady, tonight your slightest wish is my only care in this big ole' frozen world."

While Barb was pumping DJ for favors, Bobbie Lynn played out the same routine. Like sister, like sister.

Bobbie Lynn gently touched Billy's upper arm, just before getting out of the car with her sister and DJ, motioning him to place his ear near her mouth.

"Um, Billy, I don't mean to be a bother, but can you help me out with something really important?"

"Sure, Bobbie Lynn, what is it?" Billy stared, perplexed at what she wanted.

Again, Bobbie Lynn cupped Billy's ear.

"Billy, I know this sounds mean, but, once we're inside, can you be sure I'm closer to the stage than Barb? Really, Billy, it's nothing against Barb. But I wanted you to know that I'm the one who buys all the records and I'm the one with all the posters of these guys. So, since I'm the bigger music fan I think it's only fair I'm up front–like where Buddy Holly's gonna be?"

"Don't give it a second thought," he gulped, loosening the collar of his pressed linen shirt, suddenly too tight. "I'll make sure you can hear the pick hit the strings of his Stratocaster."

"Oh, Billy, thank you, thank you, thank you." She squealed, leaving a warm cherry soda-pop flavored kiss on his cheek. "I knew you were the right guy for me."

Billy drove toward the parking lot, skillfully piloting the winged beauty through streams of excited young people hurrying to the doors of the Surf for the big show, and refuge from the weather. Finding a relatively sheltered spot back by the kitchen with relief, he parked the car.

He had heard all sorts of crazy stories about the Compton twins, constantly trying to one up the other in all sorts of convoluted situations. Still, he thought it was awfully early in the evening for the identical sisters to fire up the rivalry. Either way, the blondes were stone cold knockouts. To say he was glad DJ set the whole thing up would have been a grand understatement.

The cars in the parking lot of The Surf were packed like sardines in a tin can as everyone in town was looking for something to do. Spring Break was over a month away for the Lions of Clear Lake High School and an extreme case of cabin fever had set in on the snow bound community. Cars overflowed from the venue and crowded every snow-banked side street. It seemed that everyone from miles around were nestled inside the tropical interior of The Surf, hoping to take their minds off of the miserable cold.

The Winter Dance Party Show at The Surf was the result of a canceled show at the Cinderella Ballroom in Appleton, Wisconsin, after one of the tour's buses broke down. When news hit Clear Lake that the rock and roll stars were coming to town for a fill in date, every kid in school was giddy with excitement.

Buddy Holly was the biggest thing going in rock and roll music. With Ritchie Valens and The Big Bopper along, Billy could sense it was going to be a *"show for the ages."* The last time he could remember such a ruckus was for Elvis Presley's appearance in Des Moines a couple of years earlier. The show at The Surf was not to be missed at any cost.

Cutting off Gene Vincent's *Be-Bop-A-Lula*, in mid chorus, he pulled the keys from the ignition, jumped out of the warm car and looked to the sky. Positioning a scarf around his neck, his eyes watered in the frigid air.

An Arctic blast howling through the parking lot, muffled the thud of the big Cadillac's door as he ran to open the trunk. Then, as if it were under water, its massive deck lid slowly lurched skyward. The only visible inhabitant of the empty and cavernous space was a lonely, spare Firestone tire.

A small leather case with an arm-length strap was tucked behind the spare, nearly invisible in the dark, chilly interior. Grabbing the case that housed a brand new Nagra III mobile reel-to-reel tape recorder, Billy slammed the trunk shut. Throwing the strap securely over his shoulder he made a run for the warm confines of The Surf Ballroom lobby.

The mobile recorder had just arrived after a month long wait. The miniature wonder was the prize purchased with gift money from graduating Clear Lake High School with honors and a semester early the prior December. The thought crossed his mind as he neared The Surf.

Sticking around this ice box trying to figure out where I'm going to school this fall hasn't been the best idea so far. A chance to see this show almost makes it seem like a good decision.

The words congealed his frozen thoughts as he opened the frosted over glass door of The Surf Ballroom.

"What took you so long?" DJ asked, sourly, standing at the ballroom entrance. "The show's already started!"

"What do you mean the show's already started? I don't hear any music!" Billy panicked, throwing the strap off of his shoulder and twisting to open the case.

"Calm down! I'm not talking about the music, dope. I'm talking about the Compton sisters. I swear they're about to pop a few buttons trying to get to the stage. As soon as we hit the door they took off."

"Those two are known for lovin' or fighting," Billy said, relaxing and brushing the snow out of his dark crew cut. "Guess I'm not too surprised. I think they just wanted us for the tickets."

"Ya think?" DJ shot back sarcastically. "At least we might get to watch a cat fight!"

"You're a weirdo, Evans." Billy looked over, pretending to be insulted.

"Come on man. Let's go!" DJ said turning for the Ballroom entrance.

"Wait a minute," Billy hesitated, wiping the snow from the leather case. "I wanna get this recorder set up."

"Recorder?" DJ looked on dubiously as his friend swiftly opened the case and removed three small reels. "When did you get *that*?"

Billy answered, proudly winding the tape through the recorder, meandering its way around the three and three-quarter inch reels.

"I got it Friday . . . ordered it from Sears & Roebuck about a month ago. Fifty-eight dollars. It's from Europe you know."

"Fifty-eight dollars! Who made you the King of Siam?" DJ's face puckered. Neither one of them had any money. And, what little money they did have went into their cars. "What are you recording?"

"The show." Billy stated, concentrating on the batteries in the recorder's diminutive casing.

Looking over Billy's shoulder at the miniature tape machine DJ wondered. "Couldn't you get in trouble for that? A little risky don't you think?"

"Some things in life are worth risking a little trouble." Billy brushed off the question, popping the battery cover back in place. "Besides, I'm just checking this thing out for myself. It's not like I'm going to play it on the radio or anything . . . I just need some real world experience with this baby."

"Real world?" DJ said, puzzled.

Billy rolled his eyes, embarrassed. "Annie made me record her all day yesterday reciting some awful poetry written back before toilet paper was invented."

"Little tyrant huh?" DJ grimaced, well aware of Annie Daniels' reputation.

"Whatever you do, don't let her get a hold of it," he said, pushing Billy through the door and into a thousand screaming fans as he yelled behind Billy's back, "or you'll never get it back in one piece!"

2
8:00 P.M., THE SURF BALLROOM, CLEAR LAKE, IOWA

Amidst the serene, hand painted murals of palm trees bowing down low as if praying to a sandy beach on some far off South Sea Isle, the music loving mass of young people was reaching a chaotic hysteria. Swirling blonde curls hugged feminine shoulders, severe angles of emerald, gold, and maroon ties adorned the ever-changing living sculpture.

The Surf Ballroom had been one of Iowa's historic landmarks since the 1930s. The venue hosted the big bands of Tommy Dorsey and Glenn Miller, to name just a couple. The Ballroom also proudly showed its support during the war, raising money for bonds to keep the armed forces of the United States in boots and ammunition overseas. And, it was a place where, beneath its sweltering stage lights, the embryonic rock 'n' roll careers of Bill Haley and the Comets, Carl Perkins, and many others had been nurtured. Rock 'n' Roll, found a home at The Surf Ballroom.

DJ grabbed the microphone out of Billy's hand while he concentrated on adjusting one of the recorder's controls. He tapped the microphone experimentally, bowing to his adoring fans in the lowest voice he could muster.

"Check one, check one, two!"

"Give that back to me you idiot! You're drawing attention!" Billy snapped, punching his pal in the shoulder, nearly knocking him over while retrieving the microphone.

"Owwww . . . !" DJ laughed and winced all at once. "That's going to leave a mark."

Billy tugged at DJ's coat, never taking his eye from the mini controls.

"Stand in front of me, over to the right."

"Why? I like where I'm standing. Where are the girls? I can't see 'em."

"Just do it will ya?" Billy exclaimed while positioning his friend's 6'3" 220-pound frame for proper camouflage. "Excellent!"

"Excellent what?" DJ said.

The crowd's volume, which began as a moderate murmur, now rose to pockets of wild cries, making normal conversation nearly impossible. DJ squirmed around to look behind him at Billy's face, intent on his instruments. The ever-increasing squeals, hoots, and crowd whistles were accompanied by wafting smells of hairspray, heavy cologne, and sweat mixing with sultry air.

"Just stay there," he said while adjusting the recorder's preamp, "the VU meter looks great."

"What's a VU?" asked DJ.

"You're going to make the ideal baffle DJ. This is gonna work out perfect!"

"Well whoop dee crap! I'm glad I can be of some help Thomas Edison." DJ rolled his eyes as The Big Bopper took the stage."

Ahhhh, Hello Baaaaby!

FEBRUARY 3, 12:00 A.M.,
THE SURF BALLROOM PARKING LOT

The Surf's incandescent lights cut through the relentless, biting, winter wind, clearly illuminating Barb and Bobbie Lynn's fiery faces. The two sisters scuffled ungraciously, hands moving from pointed fingers to hips, and back again, as their identical poodle skirts sharply jostled left to right.

"I TOLD you he gave it to ME!" Barb grabbed her sister's arm, clamped tightly against her midriff and tugged sharply at Bobbie Lynn's balled up fist.

"What are they fighting over anyway?" DJ wondered, rubbing his hands together, wishing he would've remembered to bring his gloves.

Billy sighed, stooping, putting his back to the wind and lighting a Marlboro Red. "It's all Buddy Holly's fault."

"What do you mean it's Buddy Holly's fault?" DJ winced while the twins verbally sparred, with ear splitting squeals and visible jabs. Car engines, aching from the assault of old man winter began sputtering to life around the Brougham.

"Well, it's actually Buddy Holly's pick's fault," he corrected himself as the smoke from his Marlboro streaked away in the angry winter tempest.

Billy couldn't get close to the stage himself, not with all the screaming girls swooning and clutching at each other, waving frantically when one of the performers swept close by.

But he could see Buddy, smiling down, gesturing to the crowd between phrases, flicking his guitar pick into the crush of ecstatic fans. Instantly, a screeching mass converged where the pick landed; hands grasping, shoving, and straining to reach the amber tortoise-shelled piece, still slippery from Buddy's sweaty fingers.

DJ dug a fifty-cent piece out of his pocket. "I'll flip ya' to see who has to go break those two up . . . deal?"

Billy took another drag from his cigarette and flicked it to the ground. "Heads I go, tails you go."

As the coin winked skyward, DJ snagged it out of the air in midflight, a gust of wind nearly blowing it to the ground.

"Heads it is . . . we have a loser." DJ announced as the twins continued to go at it. "You my friend are the referee."

"Let's go pry 'em apart." Billy sighed regretfully. "Looks like I'm gonna have to call a time out."

FEBRUARY 3, 12:20 A.M., HIGHWAY 18, MASON CITY, IOWA

Well ya got trouble my friend, trouble right here in River City, with a capital T and that rhymes with P and that . . .

"Would you shut up?" DJ scowled at Billy who was bellowing out Meredith Wilson's masterpiece playing on the radio as they made their way home from Mason City.

"It would be one thing if you could sing, but you can't. It would be another thing if you knew all the words, but you don't. So how about sparing me the pain?"

Billy was euphoric and in a singing mood as the performance at The Surf was outrageously good. Even under extremely trying circumstances, the show-must-go-on attitude of the artists, along with their comedic on stage antics, drove the crowd into a passionate frenzy.

Beside the fact that the musician's tour busses broke down, and the drummer for the evening contracted the flu, the stars of the show pitched in for one another. Ritchie played drums for Buddy and then Buddy returned the favor by playing drums for Ritchie and Dion and the Belmonts. The effort didn't go unnoticed by the crowd. Most bands would have cancelled the show at The Surf, but the extraordinary dedication of the multi-talented stars kept the show on the road.

Billy hadn't had the opportunity to listen to any of the tapes yet, but the Nagra worked perfectly. The ingenious little Swiss machine didn't hiccup a single time during the whole performance, and Billy's mind was overloaded with excitement from having completed his first recording in the field. It was, after all, why he bought the machine in the first place.

Intensely interested in all things "undercover," Billy was considering the career possibilities that the field of investigation could offer. Recording equipment was becoming smaller, and more miniaturized everyday. With the Cold War on, there were always reports of fantastic gadgets like eyeglasses that could take pictures, or recorders the size of a pack of cigarettes that could capture conversations from distances of over 30 feet away. It all intrigued the young man who could pick just about any college he wanted to go to in the fall.

He was itching to pull the car over and snatch the recorder from the trunk to take a listen, but the weather had become too bad and even more so with every slowly passing mile.

Billy picked the song back up, *"trouble with a capital P and that rhymes with T and that stands for pool!"*

"Ah good grief, cut it out." DJ grumbled, interrupting Billy's enthusiastic review. "I've had about enough for one night. Listening to those two squawk it up for the last twenty minutes was driving me crazy. Now YOU'RE gonna finish me off!"

Billy shrugged his shoulders, his cigarette making short movements, matching the jerks on the wheel as he compensated for the gusts of wind, pushing broadside on the Cadillac. What little of the road that could be seen, shone like polished onyx beneath the horizontally blowing snow, offering little visibility.

"Unlike you, it seems," Billy shot back at his friend, keeping his eyes on the road, "I can appreciate a good song."

"I know what kinda music I like, and it ain't show tunes!" DJ retorted as they passed the dull and nearly obscured lights of the airport.

"You're just mad because you didn't get to play any back seat bingo with Barb tonight."

"Back seat bingo?" DJ groused. "We couldn't even find those two 'till the show was over. I never got a cha—LOOKOUT!" DJ yelled, frantically.

Billy swerved sharply, narrowly missing the oncoming car that had crossed the double yellow line, wandering into the opposite lane. The Cadillac broke loose from the icy pavement as he yanked the steering wheel hard to the right, fishtailing wildly from one white line to the other.

"Hold on to it, Billy!" DJ yelled, grasping for the dash to steady himself as the Brougham careened again, sliding uncontrollably to the left, nearly perpendicular to the direction of the road.

"Hang on! . . . Hang on!" Billy shouted, correcting the skid a third time, shakily bringing the Cadillac to a stop in the middle of the road. "Holy Cow! That guy almost killed us!!!" Billy cursed at the taillights in the rear view mirror. "Did you get a look at it?"

DJ twisted in his seat to follow the retreating red lights, now almost obscured by a wall of blowing snow and sleet, frothing around the car's slick tires.

"It was one of those Ford station wagon tanks. If he would've hit us with that wagon, we both would've been goners."

Billy shivered in the cold cab, trying to gather himself as they sat motionless on the dark highway, the moon buried deep under the fathomless grey sky.

"Nice driving," DJ said, eyes wide like a hoot owl, "almost as good as I would have done it."

"From you I'll take that as a compliment." Billy said taking a deep breath. "DJ, it's time to get this thing off the road. Whadda ya say?"

"My sentiments exactly Billy boy."

FEBRUARY 3, 12:40 A.M., MASON CITY MUNICIPAL AIRPORT

It had been a treacherous ten mile ride on Highway 18 for the stars of *The Winter Dance Party*. The journey from Clear Lake to the Mason City Airport turned out to be more sledding than driving, with each turn posing the risk of losing life or limb.

Due to a coin toss for a seat on the plane, and an ill JP Richardson, the passenger list changed for the flight, resulting in additional paperwork that needed to be filled out. The Dwyer Flying Services representative, eager to get out of the cold, knocked quickly on the window of the 1955 Ford Country Squire wagon.

"We need signatures from the new passengers," he directed, sticking a clipboard and a pen toward the driver, crouched behind the barely opened slit in the window.

Reviewing the updated passenger sheet, the representative confirmed the changes.

"So we have Mr. Richardson flying in the seat of Waylon Jennings, Mr. Valens in place of Tommy Allsup, and Mr. Holly flying as previously arranged, any other changes?"

"That's it," the driver responded, "let's get these guy's on their way."

"OK. See you next time," the representative said in a rush, turning to make a dash for the small airport terminal. The driver silently applauded the big wagon's steelshod bulk as he opened the doors for the performers.

"Anything without the weight of this big boy and we might have found ourselves upside down in a ditch back there."

The comment went unacknowledged as the passengers scampered to get out of the car. Freezing air whipped at the performers lungs as they hauled their luggage and bags of dirty laundry from the back of the station wagon. After thanking the driver for their safe journey, they made their way to the small plane waiting to take them to North Dakota, and a warm bed for the night.

The hotel rooms reserved for them in Fargo would feel like a vacation, especially when compared to the accommodations they had to endure on the tour.

The tour was a logistical nightmare, constantly back-tracking hundreds of miles from one show to the next. Two buses had broken down, and the heaters were on the fritz in both of them. The cold was so bad during one night, that the guys from Dion's group; The Belmont's, began burning newspapers in the aisle of one of the buses just to keep from freezing. No one on the tour had any clean clothes and the food was consistently horrible. To cap it off, nearly all of the musicians suffered from the flu and some even had severe frostbite.

For the musicians in the plane, it was time to put the nightmare of being on the road behind them for a short while. As the red and white Beechcraft Bonanza sputtered to life, its passenger door was latched down tight. However, the weather conditions continued to deteriorate.

The small, four passenger plane taxied slowly toward frozen Runway #17 for take off, its lights shining steadily at each wingtip and V-shaped tail, feebly illuminating the wet, gray concrete. At negative 35 degrees wind chill, the Northern Express raged like a winter hurricane.

A voice from the terminal cracked on the radio, "You're clear for take off. Have a safe flight."

Welcome to Clear Lake. *The Town That Sails Away With Your Heart!*

The familiar, downtown welcome sign that beckoned summertime water sport enthusiasts from miles around, was half covered in snow as it drifted by the Cadillac's passenger side window. It felt good to finally be alone. After dropping DJ off and picking up his little sister Annie, who spent the evening at her best friend's house, Billy's thoughts turned wearily to a warm bed.

He could think of a million other places he would've rather been, but, if a person had to stay in Clear Lake, house sitting for his Aunt and Uncle while they were in Florida, was definitely not the end of the world. The house was huge. It had a game room with pinball machines, a pool table, and even a single-lane bowling alley. The refrigerator was stocked with pop, candy bars and White Castle frozen hamburgers. His uncle's new color television set was an added bonus as well...not Florida, but not too shabby. Billy wasn't thinking of the games he would shoot, or the rumblings of his stomach however. His thoughts swung back to the garage and what needed to be done with the car. The morning would bring a long day of cleaning and spit shining the prized Eldorado, that was for sure. Whether he would get away with it or not, given an Uncle who was known to detail his cars with a Q-tip, was definitely not, a sure thing.

The Eldorado Brougham was his Uncle's finest car. It was also Cadillac Motor Company's top of the line luxury vehicle in 1958. Earl Willingham's Cadillac was number 26 of only 196 built in '58. And, anytime he had the chance, he'd tell everyone within earshot about his, "Emerald Lady."

In the summertime, Billy recalled watching his Uncle drive the Detroit beauty with its stainless steel top shining like a diamond to the Oak Hills Country Club on Friday afternoons, ready to tackle the eighteen-hole course. In a club where the car your driving in with was almost as important as the club you drove with on the golf course, Earl's car was head and shoulders above his gin and tonic sipping pals. The other top shelf luxury vehicles parked at the club house from Ford, Packard, Desoto and all the rest, were mere imitators.

Billy's part-time job of mowing grass at Oak Hills, surrounded by the warm lake and its giant green sycamore trees, now seemed a million miles away. The frozen winter landscape that enveloped Clear Lake, and everything around the little town, now seemed like an icy cocoon.

As the frozen sidewalks rolled by, he felt a little guilty about "borrowing" the car. His uncle had specifically asked him to keep an eye on it, but he didn't say anything about driving the masterpiece. The instructions he left before heading out of town were simple, clear, and delivered from least to most important:

"Make sure you don't forget to set the trash out, and stop by the pro shop at the Country Club to pick up that new Arnold Palmer sand wedge I ordered when it comes in."

Then, he gave Billy that intense, 'Uncle Earl' look that he knew only too well. "And above all keep a close eye on my Emerald Lady. That pesky neighborhood mutt likes to sneak in the garage when no one's looking and relieve itself on the tires!"

He thrust his index finger skyward and ranted on: "One of these days I'm going to be faster than that little dog, and when that day comes, it will be the last of the indoor plumbing days for that flea bit scoundrel!"

The same index finger dropped and jabbed him straight in the chest. It was the last thing his uncle said as he tossed him keys to the castle, and the car.

Tonight thankfully, the Emerald Lady had not suffered the indiscretions of the neighborhood pooch. It had however, been soiled by the salty grime of the streets, a mid highway fish-tailing incident and two soggy poodle skirt impressions left by the near perfect rear ends of the Compton twins. The snow was up to the Caddy's rims as he pulled the car to a stop in front of his uncle's home.

"You've got to be kidding me!"

Exasperated, he looked at the long uphill driveway, completely iced over by the elements. Boxy holly bushes, lining the long ribbon of misleading smoothness, that hours before was the driveway, dared him to place rubber to pavement. The hopeless surface was cunningly hidden by powdery wisps of snowflakes.

"No way am I going to try and make it up that grade tonight."

Billy got out and peered back at the car while Annie lay inside sound asleep, her head against the frosted window.

It was painfully apparent that DJ had been right; the decision to venture the Cadillac from the cozy confines of the garage, turned out not to be a good one. Earlier in the night, it seemed harmless to drive the car to the show and leave his old '40 Ford Deluxe in the drive way. But given the current predicament he was facing, taking the Ford would have been the better idea by a long shot. Now, he wished he had done just that.

I'll get up early and shovel the driveway. Put the car in the garage and make it sparkle like the crystal in Aunt Edna's China cabinet. It'll be fine . . . just need to grab the recorder and tapes.

After the show, he tucked the recorder neatly back into the safe spot behind the spare tire, far away from the Compton's who were certainly at war and about to come to blows.

The thought that maybe he had been a little over-cautious crossed his mind as he struggled to put the key into the frozen solid lock of the Caddy's trunk. As he fumbled with the key, the wind felt more like a furnace than the frigidly cold air that it was. His predicament became apparent.

It's not going to happen. I can't risk damaging the paint on this car. I'd need a blow-torch to free this lock up tonight . . . it's out of the question.

He squinted again, trying to focus up the dim driveway. The recorder and the tapes would have to spend the night in the trunk. Growing uneasy, Billy considered the impact the extreme cold might have on the freshly captured music stored on the tapes. He prayed the recordings wouldn't suffer harm in the extreme elements. Putting the keys that were burning his gloveless hands back into his pocket, he quickly carried his sleeping sister to the house.

4

Michael?" a feminine voice softly called inside the tow truck. "It's Wanda." The Motorola radio crackled with the call from the Cerro Gordo County Police Station.

"Hey," came the exhausted voice of Michael Minton, roused from his sleep against the cab door. "I hope you're calling to tell me there's a bunk with my name on it."

"Sorry, Michael," Wanda answered, apologetically. "I know we've put you through the wringer tonight, but you know how it goes with these Severe Weather Alerts. We need you to go and do one more run."

It had been a busy night at Minton Towing. As the premier towing service for the city of Clear Lake, a Severe Weather Alert was guaranteed to result in a long, grueling, work shift.

Handling the evening's SWA was chaos for the small towing company, mainly because only half of the tow trucks that Minton employed were operating. To make matters worse, the owner of the company, and Michael's father, Fred Minton, had been home with the flu for the prior two nights. Nick Isaacs, Minton's part-time driver, was also out of the mix; snowed under in Algona, 18 miles away.

The unfortunate situation left Eddie Neal, Minton's right-hand man along with Michael, to wrangle the mess alone.

"Let's have the address, Wanda." Michael rubbed his blurry eyes and moved from a slouch to turn up the heater again. "How many have we done tonight? I lost track."

"Twelve for you and ten for Eddie, a new record." She replied with a warm smile in her voice, trying her best to find something positive to report.

"Well let's hope it's a record that never gets broken!" Michael replied with a tired laugh and signed off.

It was turning out to be one of those nights. The kind that makes a guy wonder what he's doing with his life. Especially if the guy in question is sure he could do better. Driving around town answering a never-ending stream of roadside service calls, gave Michael plenty of time to think about life, and where was headed.

Michael willingly helped out in the family business, but since his graduation from high school in 1957, he had been unable to stifle the resentment of being stuck in Clear Lake. He hated his job, and he felt like the future he wanted so badly, was slipping away from him.

Days of a brighter past shuttered through Michael's mind like a set of old film clips as he headed toward the address that Wanda gave him.

Fond memories of Drama Club Awards, and lead roles in plays and musicals at school, spun in his mind like a movie house turnstile. The articles in *The Des Moines Register* that declared: "Minton is a natural born actor . . . a star in the middle of Iowa, ready for a life in cinema if he chooses." Then there was the opportunity to go to Italy, with a chance to be an extra in William Wyler's *Ben Hur*. But, like always, money was short, so he stayed home and helped with the business.

He gunned the old International to life and swung the nose the other direction, heading back into the swirling darkness.

★★★★★★★★★★★★★★★★★★★★★★★★★★

FEBRUARY 3, 1959
A CATASTROPHE AND THE CADILLAC

★★★★★★★★★★★★★★★★★★★★★★★★★★

5
8:00 A.M., THE WILLINGHAM RESIDENCE, CLEAR LAKE, IOWA

Billy stumbled into the kitchen, intent on starting a pot of coffee as soon as humanly possible. Even the smell of it would go a long way in waking him up. Looking through the kitchen window, the lake was a solid sheet of glaring ice. He winced and looked away as the morning sun bounced shards of light from its surface through his tired eyeballs.

The waterfront home was the perfect place for Earl Willingham, owner of M&W Marine and Power Boat Company. Located just off Sunset Marina, the tall, ornate, 1897 Spanish Colonial style home was as close as some thought you could get to paradise in Iowa. This morning, as Billy sipped his coffee, the lake, surrounded by snow resembled a paradise, although a frigid one. The ice encrusted land-scape looked like it could easily be a part of some Alpine vacation spot nestled in Austria or Germany instead of Iowa.

Vacation . . . I sure hope they're having a great time.

Billy's Mom and Dad had finally, after so many years, accepted the invitation to join his Aunt and Uncle at their Florida home for a winter vacation. It was always the same story every year; his uncle would invite his parents to Florida, and every year they would decline. Always too busy, always something going on, that is until this year. Finally, Tom and Catherine Daniels decided to take advantage of the invite and go live the good life in sunny Florida for a week. The vacation was a long time coming and Billy was overjoyed that his parents were going. After all this time, they were taking a break.

He left the kitchen to yell down the hallway at his little sis, already well aware of what her response would be.

"Annie! Watcha eatin' for breakfast sweetie?"

"Raisin Bran, but pick out the raisins," a small voice came from a bedroom on the left. "Don't pour the milk yet either, I don't want it soggy and make two pieces of toast . . . crunchy."

"Butter and grape jelly?"

"Yes, but I'll put the butter and jelly on the toast myself."

Little Annie Daniels was used to getting her own way. With the reprieve from classes at Clear Lake Elementary School, caused by the bombardment of ice and snow, and the additional attention from her older brother, she was no doubt enjoying herself.

Billy knew the routine like the back of his hand and was just fine with watching Annie for the week. Agreeing that he would stay home for the task allowed his parents to feel comfortable leaving town for vacation. That alone was worth it.

Annie Daniels was a marvel. Billy had doted on his younger sister since the first time he sat next to his mother as a little boy and watched Annie sleeping as a newborn. She could be the sweetest little girl in the world and at the same time, she could be as demanding as General George S. Patton battling a division of Panzer tanks.

A very gifted child with an IQ of 140, Annie had always been special. Most times she behaved like a much older person than her tender years, and thought like one too. She'd been the geography bee winner at Clear Lake Elementary, was the captain of the Elementary Science Club, and the spelling bee champion for the last four years in a row.

Annie was smart no doubt. She was great with counting games, maps, stars, or anything that had to do with science. On the other hand, she was also good at wandering off and taking things apart that generally weren't meant to be dismantled. And, on certain occasions, she didn't always get things back together again the way they started out. The family television, a toaster or three, and Great Grandma Daniel's antique cotton gin were only a few of the victims of her curiosity. She was smart . . . but still a kid.

The diminutive Annie, barely four feet tall, emerged from the bedroom. Her footie pajamas made a soft swishing sound on the linoleum. On top of her pajamas she was dressed in her school clothes; a pair of plaid pants and a navy sweater. Her black, horn rimmed glasses that she was 'growing into,' were one size too big.

"Why are you dressed for school?" Billy asked, chuckling at her appearance. "There won't be any school . . . buses can't run in this mess. Relax a while."

Annie payed him little attention, sniffing the cereal, and eyeing the toast with skepticism. She scampered back into her room, hoping to push her IQ even higher. "I study better in my school clothes."

Meanwhile, Billy finished washing the dishes in his Aunt's white, porcelain sink. Cleaning the kitchen was not on his mind as he put the knives and forks back into the utensil drawer. Cleaning the Cadillac, and getting it back into the garage, was the top priority of the morning.

A quick shower, a bowl of oatmeal, and two winter coats later, Billy was out the door with shovel in hand, ready to clear the driveway. Caught in the fog of the morning mist, he slogged through the snow that covered his Uncle's driveway. Looking toward the street, for a moment, he thought his eyes were playing tricks on him. Through the snow-covered line of holly bushes edging the lawn, the long graceful outline of the Cadillac seemed to be absent from the street.

Picking up the pace, and nearing the bottom of the driveway just before reaching the mailbox, it was apparent that his mind wasn't playing tricks on him at all. Looking left then right, the sick feeling that comes with knowing something is terribly wrong began to settle in his stomach.

"It's got to be here!!" He yelled into the frigid morning, his voice bouncing off of the lake like a lead balloon.

Staring down at the tire divots left in the snow, all doubt was erased. Faint remnants of tire tracks zigzagged briefly before straightening out in the middle of the street, signaling that the Cadillac was in fact, gone.

With his head spinning like a top on a tilt-a-whirl, he ran to the house at breakneck speed.

No one would steal a car buried up to its axles in snow . . . especially on a night like last night. There must be an explanation!

He checked the front door, and both back doors looking for a note or citation from a towing company. He went to the garage and to the pool house door. The shell-shocked teenager found nothing but the ice cold air in his face.

Running to the spot in the Willingham driveway where his Ford Deluxe sat cold and silent, he tore open the door. Reassessing the situation, he reasoned his next move.

There are only two towing companies in town; Trinkle's Lock and Recovery and Minton's Towing.

He gave the accelerator a couple of pumps, thinking about the immediate tasks in front of him.

I've got to make sure Annie stays put . . . run down and get the car. I'll be back in less than forty-five minutes.

He turned the key.

The 221 L-Head in the old Ford had no intention of cranking over, able to muster only a machine gun style series of clicks from its solenoid.

Dead battery! He yelled, slamming his palm against the steering wheel.

Always a dead battery . . . Time to call for a lift.

DJ laughed uncontrollably upon learning of his buddy's predicament, so loud that Billy had to hold the receiver away from his ear.

"Oh, this is classic!" DJ mimicked Billy's brag from the night before. "Trust me DJ. I've got it handled."

He continued to let him have it. "The girls like it. I'll clean it up in the morning. Am I crazy, or did I hear you say all those things last night?"

"Come on! Cut me a break, pal." Billy ground his teeth, irritated by the comment. "I'm in trouble here and besides, I didn't hear much concern about the Cadillac after Barb told you she just loved how the back seat felt . . . right?"

"Yeah, well, OK. But nothing happened!" DJ continued the rant. "It was still a bad idea. You might have been one of the smartest guys in school, but as far as I'm concerned you're a knuckle-head and one wrench short of a full set! It was a Severe Weather Alert last night, you know they tow cars left on the street to make way for the salt trucks!"

"Are you going to help me or not?" Billy yelled, now fed up with his friends mouthing off. "I need a ride to Ron's Auto Parts not a speech about my decision making. If I wanted a lecture I could have just called my Dad."

"Where's the Cadillac?" DJ asked, deciding he'd applied a sufficient amount of brow beating.

"I don't know . . . couldn't find the ticket," Billy answered, agitated. "It's got to be at Trinkle's or Minton's."

"OK. I'll be there in five minutes." DJ huffed. "But it won't be in the Fairlane. I'm trying to keep it out of the snow. We'll get that old clunker of yours running."

An hour and a fresh battery later, the Ford struggled back to life, belching a tailpipe full of coal black smoke. Billy slammed the hood and the two friends made their way to the kitchen to warm up while the car did the same.

"I talked to Trinkle's and they don't have it." Billy said, setting a scalding hot cup of black coffee in front of DJ on the kitchen table. "I didn't get an answer at Minton's but it's got to be there."

"Yeah, they do most of the SWA towing anyway." DJ agreed. "If you need help cleaning up today, you know, the Caddy . . . I can lend you a hand."

The offer made Billy feel a whole lot better about the situation. He knew he was going to be up to his neck in it after all, and acknowledged the gesture.

"Thanks pal, I appreciate that. The car is going to be a mess."

After bribing Annie with the promise of bringing her a slice of chocolate cake from Mather's Market, that was as long as she agreed to stay in her room for an hour, they tore out of the front door, headed for Minton's. Finally, Billy thought he was on to a plan.

This should be simple. Get the car. Shovel the driveway and doll up the Caddy in the garage . . . end of story.

9:05 A.M. MINTON TOWING COMPANY, CLEAR LAKE, IOWA

Fred Minton was an early bird kind of guy, usually accustomed to 9:00 a.m. being mid morning . . . but not today. The smallish man, known around town for his generosity and the Kaywoodie pipe that perpetually hung from the right side of his mouth, was groggy and slow, fighting off the remnants of the flu. Still, he was thankful that at least his temperature had subsided.

Work was calling after the first of the winter storm fronts had passed, and the result was a holding yard full of towed and broken down vehicles. Each car was attached to an owner, and soon, every one of those owners would be knocking on his door, looking for their wheels.

Filing through a chain full of skeleton keys, much like a secretary would file through a Rolodex, Fred opened the door to his shop. Reaching over in front of the plate glass window, just as he'd done for the last twenty years, he flipped the sign hanging by a piece of old frayed yarn, from "Closed" to "Open."

There wasn't much moving in the cottage-like town, and the shop was quiet. Fred adjusted his suspenders, slacking from the loss of weight he suffered from the sickness and began thumbing through the towing receipts for each of the vehicles deposited in the lot by Eddie and Michael the night before. *It won't stay quiet around here for long.* He mumbled to himself.

After toggling on the small black-and-white TV set, perched on a pair of shop manuals behind his desk, the veteran tow truck driver readied for the day, reaching for the keys to open the cash drawer. Before he could turn the key, a gold wristwatch lying on the desk caught his attention. He recognized it immediately and felt a stab of unease run through his already aching body. The note stuck to the dial of the telephone with "Dad" written on the front, accelerated his anxiety. Something wasn't right.

After reading the note, he took the pipe out of his mouth, put it on the desk, and thought about his son. Hurt seeped into his every bone, knowing this day was probably coming for a long while. He had wanted to sit down and talk to Michael, tell him to follow his dreams and not to worry about him or the business anymore, but the timing never seemed to be right.

Fred knew, as any father would, that his son was trying to do the stand up thing in the business, yet how terribly his mother's death affected his young life. That kind of pain, he himself knew all too well. Caught up in his own loss, he wasn't able to muster the energy or emotion to spare for his son. It was energy he should have found, one way or the other.

The shop will always be around if you want to come back. I'm very proud of you. Go do what you want with your life, while you're still young.

Those were the words that Fred wanted to tell him. Now the opportunity to say it had passed him by. The note, and the words Michael wrote touched his heart, yet the sorrow was interrupted in a moment of clarity as he stared at the golden time piece. Gingerly, he opened the money drawer, expecting to see nothing inside but bad checks and a few dust balls. His expectations were confirmed. *Where would he go? How would he get there?*

The question swirled in Fred's mind with a million other thoughts and emotions. He had his suspicions, but Michael's car could barely make it out of town much less get him out of Iowa. His temple began a familiar, monotonous pounding as the shop door opened.

"Hey, Boss." Eddie's burly voice advanced through the doorway ahead of his swarthy arms, holding two hot cups of coffee and a box of Dixie Crème donuts. "Here ya go," he handed Fred a cup' a Joe and one of Dixie's custard filled delights, "glad to have ya back."

Fred gazed up and thanked him, his face taking on a gray, ashen pallor. Eddie had known Fred Minton for a long time and it was painfully obvious, that whatever was bothering his friend and boss, wasn't from having the flu or going without sleep.

"Eddie, Michael's gone. It looks like he left sometime early this morning."

"Do you mean leave as in quit work, or leave as in leave town?"

"Both," Fred replied.

"Well I saw Michael sleepin' in your chair at around 1:00 a.m. when I left," Eddie tried to reassure him, "he can't be too far."

"Eddie." Fred asked with a note of desperation creeping into his voice. "I'm worried about him. How would he go?"

Eddie couldn't help but feel sorry for him. He had tried his best to be there for Fred, but he wasn't much of a consoling kind of guy. He could bring coffee, talk about the high school basketball team, the weather, his dog, or the joys of a good towing winch, but that was about it. Sometimes it was enough to take Fred's mind off of his wife and sometimes it wasn't. After all he'd been through, now this.

"He'll probably come driving back here any minute," Eddie ventured, trying to keep Fred positive about the situation. "Last night was a tough shift, stressful as heck. I'm thinkin' he just needed a good night's rest."

Fred pointed through the front window, scratching the back of his neck in confusion. "His car is still in the parking lot. Do you think he could have left with a friend? Did he say anything to you about—" He stopped in mid sentence, alarmed by Eddie's bewildered stare, clearly locked on the empty tow hook of Wrecker #3.

"What is it?" Fred asked.

"Fred," Eddie stuttered turning back to his boss, "please tell me someone came in this morning and picked up the Cadillac."

A ghost white pale spread across Fred's face. His voice shook. "What Cadillac?"

In the parking lot, Billy Daniels and DJ Evans were walking toward Minton's door.

10:00 A.M., ROUTE 66, OKLAHOMA CITY, OKLAHOMA

At that same moment, Michael Minton was speeding across Oklahoma, burning up the road, stopping only for gas. Feeling guilty and liberated at the same time, he pushed the events of the past several hours to the back of his mind, intent on staying focused on his deliverance from Clear Lake.

The Caddy was flying at over 80 miles an hour down the highway, but he had not managed the courage to open the glove compartment, revealing the owner of his get away car. For the moment, he was free and driving as fast as he could. The great American west, and all of his dreams, lay ahead. A green Cadillac Eldorado was the way to get there.

The music was over.

The applause of admiring fans, shouting from the ballroom floor was gone. Only the deputy sheriffs hurried footsteps broke the still, low lying ground fog covering the frozen cornfield.

Gasping and out of breath, the deputy frantically slogged through the snow, desperately trying to reach a fractured aircraft spotted earlier by an air search.

Finding the plane lying helplessly against a mangled barbed wire fence, the eerie silence tells him all he needs to know. Along with the luggage and scattered clothes on the ground, and within the lifeless and twisted wreckage that once was Dwyer Flight Services N3794N, there are four young men.

There will be no rescue. There is no one to save.

10:05 A.M., MINTON TOWING COMPANY, CLEAR LAKE, IOWA

Can I help you?" Fred answered the door, immediately recognizing Billy as the son of Tom Daniels, manager of M&W Marine. M&W was a steady customer and his father had called on Minton to haul countless boats around central Iowa for the large Marine dealer.

"Hello, Billy." Fred managed a smile.

"Hello, Mr. Minton. It's good to see you." Billy replied. "We're looking for my uncle's Cadillac. There was a goof-up last night and we think it's been towed here."

Fred cast a glance at Eddie.

"Was it a new Cadillac?" Eddie asked, avoiding eye contact with Billy, "a real nice light green color?"

"Yep, that's the one!" Billy exhaled with relief.

Fred's pallor deepened further. He shook his head, and palmed his Kaywoodie pipe. "Sit down boys, we've got a problem."

The teenagers sat in the office while Fred and Eddie explained the situation. Billy was slack jawed, unwilling to believe what he was hearing.

This can't be happening. Billy moaned, staring at the wall like a zombie. The world went silent, his agony interrupted only by the flickering TV sitting on Minton's roll top desk.

Promotional pictures of the Big Bopper, Ritchie Valens, and Buddy

Holly appeared on the small green tinted screen. Billy's thoughts drifted to the show the prior evening. It had lived up to its billing and more.

He knew the show would make the papers the next day. The fact that morning television was talking about it was really no surprise. It was a great experience . . . but the car?

The momentary reprieve from the serious situation at hand was interrupted by a special report from KGLO-TV in Mason City. The confusing film footage darted back and forth on the little television in the shop. The local police seemed to be scrambling around in a cornfield with what looked like a small downed aircraft. Someone was yelling his name.

"Bill." DJ's voice cut through his musings.

"What?" He responded angrily, immersed in the distraction of the television, taking his mind off of the disastrous morning.

The sadness on his friends face was painfully clear. The last time he had seen that expression was when DJ's grandfather died.

"Do you know what's happened?" DJ asked.

"Hell yes I know what's happened," Billy shot back, "my Uncles' car has been stolen and I am in it deep."

DJ shook his head weakly, barely able to speak.

Eddie bit his lip as he looked down at Billy, reporting what he heard on the radio earlier.

"I'm sorry son but Buddy Holly, Ritchie Valens, The Big Bopper,

Tommy Allsup and their pilot got killed in a plane crash outside of town last night."

Billy stood up, knocking his chair over as he fell backwards, looking for something to hold on to. Knees shaking with beads of sweat suddenly appearing around his temple, he ran for the parking lot as fast as he could. His morning oatmeal was coming up fast.

Billy stomped around the frigid lot, kicking the tires on the Ford and pounding his hands on its hood. In his mind, the show he saw just hours earlier began to rerun in flashes. The smiles on the performer's faces, the musical acrobatics and the fun on stage.

Their friendliness was contagious and the feeling carried over to an appreciative crowd that loved every second of it. The performers made it a night that no one would ever forget. It was magic. Now, in an instant, that magic was gone.

How could this happen? He shouted angrily to the heavens, his clinched fist jabbing at the sky. *You've made a big mistake today!*

It was all terribly wrong, yet there was nothing he could do. He was helpless, just like everybody else.

His kicking and jabbing turned into pacing. The pacing turned into walking, rutting circles in the snow while he tried to get a grip on something, anything.

Then, a thought careened through the clouds spinning in his head. His pace slowed. The loss of the Cadillac had simply controlled his every thought. The theft of the car seemed like a calamity only a few moments ago. Suddenly, his predicament with the vehicle telescoped into a single blip, a local story in a newspaper column while world events raged all around. The knowledge came with a sadness and soberness that tugged at his heart.

An image began to consume him and it didn't have anything to do with a Cadillac, or his uncle. The tapes he made from the night before had not roused a solitary thought all morning. Now, they were all he could think about.

THE TAPES! . . . WE'VE GOT TO FIND THOSE TAPES!

He walked back into the office, brushing off the streaks of snow, piled on his shoulders

The solid can-do disposition that he was known for began to return slowly as the realities of the moment sunk in. He was in serious trouble, and there would be time to grieve the talented musicians that lost their lives . . . but now, was not that time.

All that mattered was finding that car and getting those tapes back. If something had not already happened to the tapes he made of Buddy, Ritchie, and The Bopper, the recordings would hold the last music they would ever make.

Billy searched Fred's face, taking his seat again at the desk. The tow truck driver's hands wearily rubbed at his forehead, sub-merged in his own punitive reflections. There wasn't any point in coming down on Fred. It wasn't his fault after all.

In Clear Lake, everyone knew most everyone else. Billy not only knew Michael Minton, the two were actually high school friends at one time. Michael was a couple of years ahead of Billy, yet everyone in his sophomore class, and every other class for that matter knew who he was. His acting abilities were well known and documented. If there was a school play or a local theater production it would've been hard to miss Michael Minton. From *Macbeth* to *The Bus Stops Here*, Michael always had the lead role.

In the second half of the school year, Michael and Billy even shared an elective class together in Latin. Billy remembered that Michael spoke of nothing but the movies and acting, hoping that somehow learning Latin might help his career. After that final semester, they never had a reason to spend time together.

Earlier while Billy was out in the parking lot emptying his stomach, Eddie, Fred, and DJ went over the office with a fine-toothed comb, looking for answers. The office yielded nothing but the note stuck to the phone. An empty oil drum that doubled as a trash can, sitting beside the door leading out of the shop, proved to be a little more helpful.

Nestled in the bottom of the battered tin drum was the carbon copy of a towing ticket. The details were clear:

```
             Make: Cadillac
        Model: Eldorado Brougham
        Year/Plate: 1958-XD4900
              Color: Green
          VIN: #37592005594M7S
 ADDRESS: 9312 South Shore Dr. Clear Lake
         State: IOWA EXP: 10/59
        Time of Towing: 12:50AM
```

DJ scrutinized the ticket, sighing as he handed it to Billy.

"Pretty much tells us what we already know."

Billy glanced at it briefly then gave it to Fred.

"I guess we should go the police Billy," he said with a tired voice, looking up from the ticket.

Fred sagged in his chair, momentarily staring at the floor, fully aware of what was going to happen to Michael once the authorities were called. As a father, he didn't want that for his son, arguing within himself that he was responsible for the whole mess in the first place. It wasn't true, but it seemed that way at the moment.

"I appreciate you're concern and honesty," Billy smiled, knowing that Fred was completely unaware of the recordings, "but I want to talk about some other options."

Billy knew that calling the authorities was the logical thing to do. He also knew that sometimes the best choice wasn't always the logical one, or so his granddad used to say.

If they notified the police, a call would go out to the officers on patrol. The theft wasn't a life or death situation it was just a stolen car, and there was no telling what kind of response they might get. With a Cadillac like the Brougham, there was a chance the law might come across it simply because it was so recognizable. But given the weather conditions, and the time that passed already, there was a greater chance they wouldn't come close to finding it. With the police involved, either way it turned out, Michael Minton's life would be ruined for years. Felony car theft wasn't good any way you stacked it up. Neither of the two scenarios worked out so well for Billy either. However the crisis came out in the wash, there would be the devil to pay. They needed a plan.

"Michael couldn't have left town any earlier than the time he listed for towing the Caddy." Billy rubbed the back of his neck, trying to compile the information they knew for sure. "Eddie you said you saw him around 1:00 a.m.?"

"Yeah, about then." He answered.

"He's been gone ten hours at most." DJ figured, glancing back at Billy.

Fred was sitting at his desk, listening to the boys while trying to rationalize the whole situation, admiring them for trying to come up with a solution. His mind wondered, drifting in and out of the conversation, his eyes fixed on the tack board attached to the wall behind his desk. They had turned the shop upside down, yet something was missing.

I can't put my finger on it. Fred grimaced, diverted by the anomaly.

What is it?

"Mr. Minton." Billy said, trying to get his attention.

"Sorry, Billy," he said apologetically, "I was just trying to remember something."

"Would you have any idea where Michael could have gone?"

Fred said heavily, "I think he's going to California; Hollywood to be exact. He always wanted to follow that dream."

"Does he know anybody in the film business out there?"

"Not that I've ever heard about."

"Friends or acquaintances?"

"Never mentioned anything to me about it," he looked down dejected, "sorry I'm not being much help."

Eddie, listening to the conversation from across the room, polished off his fourth Dixie Crème donut of the morning, glad that the waitress sold him on the idea of buying the jumbo box. Washing down the last morsel with a gulp of coffee, he piped up.

"Michael used to talk about some place out west now and again that had something to do with the movies, said he always wanted to go visit." He pointed toward the desk..."tacked a postcard of the place up there on the board."

Fred straightened with an air of enlightenment on his face. *That's what's missing!*

DJ noticed Fred's interest first. "What is it, Mr. Minton?"

"It may be nothing," he answered with more strength in his voice, "but the postcard that Eddie's talking about isn't on the tackboard anymore. I knew something was missing. I look at that tackboard everyday."

"Where was the postcard from?" Billy asked.

"A hotel somewhere in the Southwest," Fred strained to remember... "pretty sure it was on Route 66."

"What's the significance?" DJ pressed.

"It belonged to his mother. She stayed at the place a long time ago when she was out West, gave it to him when he was just a boy."

"Got any information about the place?" Billy wondered.

Fred wrinkled his brow. "Only that she said it was a place where movie stars stayed or something to that effect. His mother always filled his head with dreams of the southwest and the movies."

Billy leaned in. "Do you remember the name of the place by any chance?"

"No, I'm sorry Billy I don't." Fred shook his head apologetically. "I just never paid much attention to it. It had something to do with a ranch I believe."

Great. A ranch in the Southwest. DJ mumbled to himself, *there's gotta be a million of 'em out there.*

"You said it was on Route 66?" Billy continued.

Fred nodded. "I'm fairly sure about it, yes."

Billy got up and began pacing the garage floor.

His mother, he surmised. *Michael wouldn't drive right past the place on his way to California without stopping. This hotel, whatever it's called, must be important.*

Coming to a stop, he cast an eyeball in DJ's direction.

The two had known each other so long they could practically read each other's mind.

Was it possible? DJ thought. *Could they get on the highway, catch up with Michael*

and get the car back to Clear Lake by the time Billy's Uncle got home?
. . . maybe.

It sounded a bit far-fetched, but the choices were clear, and none of them offered what a guy might call an obvious solution. Only one path gave any of them a chance at getting out of the mess; they had to find the car themselves.

"Well, Tiger." DJ spoke up, breaking the silence. "I've got nothing to do in Clear Lake other than to freeze my butt off. We can roll in the Fairlane right now. I've got your back."

Billy turned to Fred, who was obviously confused by the comment.

"We want to go after him," he said flatly, "if we're able to find Michael, I'm sure we could work this thing through without getting the police involved."

Billy stopped and glanced over at DJ, who nodded his head.

"Mr. Minton," Billy cleared his throat, "there's another issue we haven't told you about...

Billy told Fred the whole story about the tapes in the trunk of the Cadillac. Eddie sat nearby, dumbfounded by Billy's streak of bad luck.

Fred admired the boys for trying to help his son, but knew that Billy was in a pickle too. He marveled sickly at the situation . . . *Michael has no idea about the tapes.*

Stealing the car was one thing, but losing those tapes was a whole other ball of wax. Given what happened earlier in the morning at Juhl's farm, he *had* to help Michael . . . *and* Billy.

Pushing himself awkwardly out of his chair, Fred walked slowly to the company safe. Spinning the numbers on the Diebold lockbox, the combination tumbler snicked open. He pulled out two stacks of fifty-dollar bills; all that remained of the company's cash reserves.

It would cost much more than the wad of fifties to keep his son from going to jail, and it certainly wouldn't keep the theft off of his permanent record. He would take the chance being offered by Billy. After all, it was the best he could hope for with every other option appearing bleak. He began to feel hot again, his temperature starting to rise.

"If you can't find him we'll call the law," he said, handing the money to Billy as he walked them to the door, "I'll do anything I can for you boys back here, you can count on that."

Billy stuffed the fifties into his coat pocket. The die was cast. The deal was done. Billy and DJ walked into Minton's looking for a car, they were walking out, trying to make the best of a bad situation.

10:45 A.M., MINTON'S PARKING LOT

The Ford idled lowly in the parking lot as the two friends sat motionless, staring at the snow falling on 7th Avenue.

Bob Hale, the Disc Jockey for KRIB radio played Buddy's "Raining In My Heart" as Billy mumbled an inaudible prayer for all that lost their lives in the crash. In shock, they tried to comprehend what just occurred and the position they now found themselves in.

Hale keyed the microphone long enough to give what few details he knew about the tragedy and a weather update. Another front was moving in from the North and schools were expected to be closed for the rest of the week. The bitter temperatures the town endured for the last two weeks were to continue.

Then, the emotional disc jockey, who served as the master of ceremonies during the show at The Surf, played *We Belong Together* by Ritchie Valens.

Finally Billy spoke. "A motel that's a ranch," he rubbed his chin in thought, "that's our best shot."

"Agreed." DJ shook his head. "I'm sure there's a zillion motels on Route 66. Information on any of them won't be easy to come by in Clear Lake. We're behind the eight ball and the clock's ticking."

"We're gonna need to talk to Annie first." Billy said, suddenly energized to move forward again. "Let's agitate the gravel and head south before we get caught in that front. We've lost enough time already."

7
1:00 P.M., IOWA STATE HIGHWAY 69 SOUTH

You are aware that you'll owe me big time, right?" DJ posed the question, raising a crooked eyebrow as they roared down Highway 69, his Fairlane covered in salt and slush.

"Yeah, I got it." Billy responded impatiently, straightening his red jacket and running his fingers nervously through his dark brown hair.

DJ lifted his ice cold Coca Cola. "I'll remember you said that. In fact I'll remember it for about fifteen car washes, a pile of oil changes, and maybe a tire rotation or two."

"I've got it. You made your point. I'll take care of it." Billy said annoyed, his ice blue eyes flashing. "Let's get this thing down the road already. The Cadillac's gettin' away."

"Simmer down, boss," DJ chuckled. "I'm just yankin' your chain. Told you I had your back, didn't I?"

"Yeah, as a matter of fact you did." Billy replied.

A serious note struck in DJ's voice after trying to lighten the atmosphere in the car. "I'm here to help you get those tapes and the Caddy, whatever it takes. Besides, I can change my own oil and I'm better at washing cars than you are."

"Thanks," Billy rolled his eyes, "I guess."

"Cool." DJ said shortly, his voice full of determination. "Let's go find that land yacht."

As he piloted the car with ease down the snowy highway, Billy hunched up against the window with a new pillow from his uncle's house.

"I'm gonna pile up some Zs," he said, "I'll pick it up after we hit 65 to Missouri."

"I've got it covered," DJ cracked. "Snooze away."

Billy made good use of the time and knocked off almost immediately, already drained from the day's events. Annie had agreed to come along without hesitation, that is after she made Billy go back to Mather's Market and get that chocolate cake he forgot to bring her.

In deep-reading mode with her new book, *Stars and Constellation's-An Advanced Guide,* she nestled herself into a cozy spot under a blanket, happy as a clam.

DJ laughed as Eddie Cochran's *Summertime Blues* played on KRIB.

We're about as far from summertime as it gets . . . a song will have to do for now.

DANNY WHITE

5:00 P.M., STATE ROAD 65 SOUTH, BUFFALO, MISSOURI

During the drive through central Missouri, mile after mile, the perilous snow and ice melted away. The late afternoon turned a brittle yellow as the cold sun reflected from the neatly piled lines of dirty snow following the curve of the road.

Winding back and forth, in perfect symmetry with the highway, the handiwork left by the scraping trucks seemed to go on forever.

It was turning out to be an easy ride. Annie had fallen asleep miles ago and DJ was enjoying the silence in the car. He was alone with only the roar of the motor and the sound of the Fairlane's tires on the road, reminiscing about the car he was driving. The car was a gift, yet something he worked hard for at the same time. His Uncle Jim was the one he had to thank for his wheels.

Jim Schroeder was a scrappy mid-western racing man who could drive the daylights out of anything with a steering wheel attached to it. He could drag race, boat race, and run the circle tracks, dirt or asphalt. While he ran at many venues, his true passion was racing in the United States Auto Club's open wheel Three-Quarter Midget series. Able to take advantage of his car building ability in the USAC Series, Jim became a local champion.

DJ grew up watching his hero run at big raceways, fairground speedways, and little hometown tracks. He adored his uncle, and Jim Schroeder returned the sentiment.

It was common to see little DJ at the steering wheel on his Uncle Jim's lap during off days at the track, while his dad, manning the camera from the pit area, never missed an opportunity to snap a photo of the next Wilbur Shaw.

Like many small town kids, DJ was always short on money but long on work ethic. The son of a secretary and a father who was in the farming business, he was accustomed to working for what he got. With his size, DJ wasn't scared of much, and certainly not of hard work.

When his uncle invited him to his garage a few days before his 16th birthday, DJ was a little more than excited. The birthday meant the family had another driver coming into the fold, and it wasn't to be taken lightly.

When he walked into the garage and his Uncle Jim yelled "Happy Birthday!" DJ wasn't quite prepared for what was sitting in the middle of the floor.

There, under the fluorescent lights of Jim's shop, was a 1956 Ford Fairlane Victoria. It wasn't quite ready to go burn up the drag strip however. In pieces, with large chunks of the car leaned up against the walls, the Fairlane looked like someone had dropped a hand grenade in the middle of it, flinging the car in a 360 degree circle around the shop. Cardboard boxes stuffed with pistons, weather stripping, pieces of interior, and a myriad other parts were stacked haphazardly around; a set of tires wobbled uncertainly nearby.

It was just what he was hoping for...a chance to build a car with his Uncle.

"What do you think of it buddy?" The proud uncle asked his favorite nephew, a grin splitting his face from ear to ear.

For the tough, hard scrabble Iowa farm kid, who had always been a playful loudmouth with some sort of wise crack ready at the end of his tongue, the gift left him speechless. Struggling to keep his emotions together, he could only muster, "Thank you Uncle Jim. It's the best gift I've ever received. I won't forget it." It was all Jim Schroeder needed to hear.

The duo rolled up their sleeves and went to work in the summer of 1957. Over the next few months and throughout the following winter, Jim shared with him the story about finding the nearly new Fairlane in a junkyard in Sioux City after a call from one of his racing pal's.

Jim retold the story one day when they were pounding a dent out of the Vicky's driver's side front quarter panel.

"The guy said it flipped a few times and landed up against a telephone pole, but it's got low mileage! When I got to the salvage yard to take a look at her, she had the crankshaft slammed into the transmission and the drive line was snapped in two. It was the ideal car! For $250 dollars cash, who could argue?"

During their quest to make the car whole again, they picked up a perfect power plant for the rebuild; a Paxton supercharged 312 cubic inch Ford Y-block. They spent days on end, wrenching and metal pounding, fueled by gallons of "garage" coffee at all hours of the morning. It seemed to take forever, but the beautiful lines of the Fairlane were slowly beginning to re-emerge.

The once mangled and nearly bent in half automobile was a sight to behold when DJ pulled it out of the garage in August of 1958. The chrome reversed wheels shined against the two-tone Raven black and yellow paint job, accented with racing stripes. The new black tuck and roll interior was the perfect touch to finish off the car. DJ remembered telling his uncle that the Vicky reminded him of a really mean Bumble Bee.

"Yeah," his Uncle replied, "a King Bee." The name stuck.

The next weekend DJ and Jim drove the Fairlane to the drag strip in Great Bend, Kansas. It was time to see what it could do. The converted runway at Great Bend was one of the best places to wring out a car in the central United States. After two passes with an elapsed time of 13.25 and 13.18 seconds respectively, he turned in a 13.15 second quarter-mile time on his last pass, bettering both he, and his uncle's expectations.

After a year of joyful automotive resurrection, they drove back to Clear Lake triumphantly in one of the fastest street cars in central Iowa.

5:45 P.M., U.S. ROUTE 66, SPRINGFIELD, MISSOURI

The lights of Springfield began to flicker in the distance. DJ down shifted the Fairlane into third gear and struck up his best megaphone voice: "Bill Daniels, calling Mr. William Thomas Daniels to the driver's seat . . . next stop, Springfield, Missouri, on world famous Route 66."

"Route 66?" The drowsy passenger mumbled in confusion, still half asleep. "Holy cow! I thought we were going to tag team this thing. You should've woken me up."

DJ flipped on the right-hand turn signal just before taking the Springfield exit.

"I was in a groove. Besides, the beautiful roar of the road covered up your obnoxious snoring the whole way."

"You don't like my snoring, you don't like my singing. Evans, I'm beginning to think you just don't like me very much." Billy concluded with a grin.

DJ laughed, slapping him on the back. "As long as you keep your mouth and your nose shut, I like you fine."

"Very funny, you're a regular Milton Berle." Billy stretched his neck from side to side, trying to get his senses back, "now how about a hamburger and a Coke?"

"I can do that." DJ said, upbeat, guiding the car off of the highway. "We'll need to get gas anyway . . . 28 cents at this exit, 30 at the last one. Wanna fill 'er up?"

Billy handed him a five dollar bill as the car came to a stop.

"Yeah, before it goes up again. They want an arm and a leg for gasoline these days."

Annie was doing an excellent job at keeping DJ on edge while Billy was dozing. After demanding a U.S. map at the last rest room break, shortly after waking up, Annie began spitting out questions like a Tommy Gun spits out bullets. How far is it to the next mile marker? Where's the next restaurant? How fast will this thing go? Can I sit up front? Tired of the endless questions, DJ reached into the glove compartment and grabbed his Breitling stopwatch, securely hung at the end of an old piece of leather shoestring.

"Here you go sweetheart, put this around your neck." He swung the watch around to the back seat, laying it in her small hand. "With this little guy and that map, you can figure out just about anything a person could ever want to know about distance and speed."

"Wow! This is so boss!" Her eyes gleamed as she looked over the retired Air Force timepiece carefully. "I'm going to time everything!"

"Great." DJ applauded, "I only ask that you don't try and take it apart, ok?"

"Sure, I wouldn't think of it." She answered, never taking her eyes off of the precise marching movements of the tiny watch hands.

As DJ walked toward Red's Giant Hamburg restaurant, he cautioned himself:

Sure she wouldn't think of it.

7:45 P.M., U.S. ROUTE 66, OUTSIDE OF TULSA, OKLAHOMA

Billy had been driving for about two hours, barreling down Route 66. The Platters *Twilight Time* whispered from the radio as its small, dull yellow light blinked in the dash.

The lore of the vast asphalt trail they called the mother road, connecting Chicago to California filled up Billy's fertile imagination. Stories about bizarre natural landmarks, and chronicles of rough and tumble cowboys danced around in his head. If a guy was lucky, he was told, he might even see a cowpoke or two riding through the western desert, driving thousands of cattle to some lonely river down Mexico way.

The road seemed to be full of stories about the Native-American Indian peoples along the way and endless tall tales of strange roadside oddity shops that dotted the 2,448-mile stretch of highway.

The knot in Billy's insides eased somewhat as the Fairlane rumbled through the wheat fields of Oklahoma. Startling visions would occasionally appear without notice along the road; a garish frying pan surrounded by flashing lights with an arrow pointing to a greasy spoon in the middle of nowhere. Giant oil rigs five stories tall would instantly sprout from a field while cattle meandered around their concrete bases. A colossal barn had its broadside painted with a fedora-topped gangster, pointing meaningfully down the road while advising; "Stop and see some of the finest automobiles of days gone by . . . take a picture inside Al Capone's 1925 Packard Phaeton! A splendid time is guaranteed for all!"

That sounds like a good time, he mused.

As the white lines of the highway flickered hypnotically beneath the wheels, his thoughts drifted away, wondering how things must have been when times were simple. Back when telephones were a luxury and folks got their news from the radio or their neighbor, instead of the television.

Back when people visited each other on a Sunday afternoon and rocking chair conversations on the front porch were a highlight of the day. The summer breezes tickled your hair while sipping a glass of lemonade . . . when lemonade was made from lemons and cars weren't simply a mode of transportation to be used and cast aside after a few too many miles. They were pieces of art.

His fascination with old cars had a long history, and he knew just where the fascination came from. With nothing but the open road ahead, he found himself thinking about the man that had meant so much in his young life and that he missed terribly; Granddad George.

George Daniels was born in 1892 in Garner, just a few miles from Clear Lake, the son of an Iowa wheat farmer. Like most boys born into a life of working the land, George was expected to support the farm. His chores ranged from ringing chicken necks for dinner, to filling troughs from the aging water truck for the livestock. He became a crack shot at shooting rats out of feed bins with his .22 rifle, catching stray goats, and an expert at repairing and maintaining the machinery of the farm. On the Daniels farm, there were plenty of machines to keep up with.

There were large, steam powered threshers, pulled by horses with wickedly curved interlocking wheels that simultaneously cut and tossed the grown wheat into neat sheaves. The mechanical water pumps that took water from the canals and distributed it to ditches along the fields, always posed a challenge. And then there was his favorite, the brand new Ford horseless carriage that their neighbor housed in the barn for the winter. He spent hours ogling the contraption, studying its parts, mystified and inspired by the engineering feat that it took to build it.

Spurred on by his love for machinery, George took a part-time job at Purcell's Machine Shop in Garner, in 1914, doing repair work to make extra money outside the farm like a lot of folks did in the area.

Not long after he began working for Purcell, a tall, stiff-looking man in a dark, three-piece suit walked into the shop, dropped a box of parts on the service counter and rang the bell a few times. Young George Daniels presently appeared from the back, wiping a thick layer of axle grease from his hands.

The man announced in a slight German accent. "I've tried all day to find someone around these parts that knows how to grind the correct angle on these valves. No one seems to know how to do it!" He eyed George impatiently. "Is your boss around? I need someone to look at these."

George, already 21 was somewhat insulted and retorted quickly. "The owner of the establishment is out right now but I can do what needs be done."

Surprised by the young man's confidence, the gentleman asked him a few technical questions, and listened carefully to his easy responses.

"Fine," the gentleman made his decision. "I'll be back at 5:00 p.m."

George produced a blank claim slip, indicating with a nod to the gentleman that pertinent billing information was needed.

"In whose name shall I make this out to sir?"

"Fred Duesenberg. Duesenberg Automobile Company."

That day was to change his Grandpa's life forever. George had never heard of Duesenberg, yet by instinct, knew the person who just left him a box full of engine parts was a man of great importance.

Mr. Duesenberg returned precisely at 5 p.m. to pick up and inspect the parts.

"Let's see if the work measures up to the talk." Duesenberg said coolly before going over each piece with surgeon-like scrutiny, inserting each valve in and out of the cylinder head he'd brought with him. Astonished and impressed by the precision of the work, he turned to George, informing him seriously.

"My brother August and I have plans to launch an automobile man-ufacturing operation here in Garner, we could use a man like you."

It was an easy decision for George. He worked for the Duesenbergs, and later the Duesenberg/Cord Automobile Company for the next 24 years. From the company's startup in Garner, through the Brothers' move to Minneapolis and finally to Indianapolis, Indiana, George was there every step of the way. Among the many highlights of his career, one included being a part of the team that produced the Bugatti U-16, one of the greatest motors of all time.

The giant Bugatti was the first motor to incorporate two straight-eight engines, mounted to a common crankcase and geared to a sin-gle drive. The ingenious invention generated enough horsepower to qualify it as the most powerful motor in the world and some very important people in high places were taking notice. When the Duesenberg's were recruited to refine the motor for the U.S. Military, George was right in the middle of it all. His in-depth knowledge of the motor's side-valve set up was indispensable to the company.

Involvement in World War I seemed to be inevitable for the United States, prompting increased interest in the Bugatti motor design for use in U.S. military aircraft. The vaunted motor allowed a shaft to be mounted between its opposing cylinder banks, allowing a gun to be fired through a propeller. Not a bad motor to have around in a war . . . a war that was coming for George Daniels.

In June of 1917, George's draft number came up. He was ready to fight for his country. The Duesenberg's on the other hand, after learning that George had been drafted, weren't so keen on the idea of losing one of their most talented machinists, especially when there were aircraft engines to build.

When Fred Duesenberg impressed on the Army that George's talents were needed at home, the military brass determined that George would be of more use to the military at Duesenberg than on the battlefield. And so, George fought World War I from the Duesenberg factory floor.

After the war he traveled to Daytona Beach with the company to work on "The Doozy" that set a new land speed record of 156 mph on the Florida sand. The following year he worked with Jimmy Murphy, who piloted his Doozy to victory in the Grand Prix of France, leaving Europe's elite motor cars behind as if they were spoiled caviar.

When the Duesenberg Empire faded in 1937, George moved his family back home to Iowa with his wife and only son, 14-year old Thomas. With troubled times in Europe and talk of a new World War, he decided that Iowa was the place to be for his family.

The year 1941 brought good times for the Daniels. It also brought bad times, not only for their family but the entire nation. There was joy when Billy was born, and outrage when the Japanese bombed the U.S. Naval base at Pearl Harbor, Hawaii. The aftershocks of the attack on the small island, eventually found their way to small towns all over America like Clear Lake, as world conflicts always seem to do.

In 1942, at the train station in Rock Island, Illinois, Tom Daniels kissed his wife and infant son goodbye, and shipped out for the war in Europe with "The Fighting First." In the 1st Infantry Division, under the Command of Major General Terry Allen, he would fight the Nazi's from North Africa all the way to the Battle of the Bulge in the Ardennes Forest of Belgium. He wouldn't see his son again until the summer of 1945.

While Billy's Dad was overseas fighting the war, George stepped in, playing a major role in raising his grandson. The two became inseparable. Grandpa Daniels had hundreds of stories and adventures of conquests with the Duesenbergs to share with the infant Billy, who could only stare up at his grandfather and listen. Tales of hair raising races, exotic journeys, and feuds between racecar drivers would distract a young Billy with an aching tooth or ease him into sleep after a trying day.

Sometimes he would go on for hours, talking to his sleeping Grandson to take his mind off of the war his son was fighting and the danger he was in.

Grandma and Grandpa Daniels were a constant support team in the Tom Daniels home, their presence as natural and comforting as the gas lamps burning steadily in the "company room" at night. Hours seemed to pass like a summer breeze through their front porch screen door when Grandpa George was around.

I wish I could talk to him just one more time. Billy thought sadly. Refocusing abruptly on the road in front of him, the highway that earlier had sparked his wild imagination, now seemed cold. A small, metal sign showing "Amarillo 115 miles" sped past while his warm childhood memories faded away into the shadowy night.

8

9:00 P.M., THE BLUE HORIZON MOTEL, CLEAR LAKE, IOWA

Civil Aeronautics Board investigator Andrew Norris was in charge of the investigation team in Clear Lake, arriving at the crash site around noon, shortly after his early morning flight from Des Moines. The investigator had been at the garish scene for nine solid hours taking photos, collecting relevant weather reports, talking to witnesses, and attempting to sort out the details of the crash.

A small, perpetually worried-looking man, Norris, who was dressed in a creased, poorly fitting gray suit, was thankful the long day had nearly come to an end. The warm motel room and cup of hot chocolate felt like heaven after battling the bracing cold air and rock-like snow of the wreckage laden cornfield.

Norris, who was a careful and thorough perfectionist, took his role as sleuth seriously. He paced his hotel room, even more uptight than usual. Knowing that the crash involving the performers was drawing world wide attention, he exacted even more care than normal in scrutinizing each piece of evidence. The investigator took obsessive notes, plotting the entire landscape of the crash, sweating every detail while recording his analysis by a hand held dictation recorder for backup.

Surrounded by mounds of paperwork, he carefully cataloged and itemized all of the various documents, annotating where each had originated from, and by whom. He pursed his lips and made a clucking noise at the back of his throat as he zeroed in on his first day summary of the crash. He'd seen this situation many times before.

Bad weather, a young pilot, and passengers needing to get somewhere quickly, making poor choices. However, this crash was different in many ways. Already there were wild rumors circulating about the accident that were proving to be distractive and highly unhelpful. Speculation that a hand gun was on board the small plane, and theories that Buddy Holly was actually flying the aircraft, were only a couple of the disconcerting new twists. He turned away from the evidence.

Ah well, it's not for me to draw conclusions yet. I just need all the information I can get . . . look at all the angles. It never hurts to be too careful.

Balanced atop the nearest stack of documents yet to review, and sitting on his Motel room floor, was the gaggle of information that he requested from Monday night's show at the Surf Ballroom. He sighed . . . the list was long.

These calls will have to wait until the morning. Right now I need a hot shower and a warm bed.

THE LAST ROCK AND ROLL SHOW

FEBRUARY 4, 2:00 A.M., THE EL RANCHO HOTEL, GALLUP, NEW MEXICO

Angling the Cadillac into a parking space at The El Rancho Hotel, Michael shut down the engine, closing his eyes in the sudden quiet. The El Rancho's neon lights were dark and there wasn't the slightest stir in the warm, dry desert air.

Finding the hotel mailbox, Michael retrieved a small, silver key with the Number "3" stamped on a blue plastic boot-shaped tag. Pleased with himself by having the foresight to call and make the reservation from a rest stop in Tucumcari, he turned toward his room.

He was still in his work uniform, and it didn't take long to carry in his things: a white T-shirt and a pair of blue jeans that was lying around at the shop. The black leather jacket and the clothes he was wearing rounded out his wardrobe. He would need more stuff, but for now, the exhausting 1,300 mile drive and the events of the last day, had left him with the singular thought of getting some rest. He shut the door, sank into the bed, and was asleep in seconds.

★★★★★★★★★★★★★★★★★★★★★★★★★★★★

FEBRUARY 4, 1959
ROUTE 66 AND A CHICKEN DINNER

★★★★★★★★★★★★★★★★★★★★★★★★★★★★

For nearly an hour, Agent Norris methodically worked through the names on the Will Call list, the employee list, and the stage support staff roster of the Surf Ballroom. The effort paid off.

One of the names on the list, Ray Robertson from Waterloo, said he ran into someone in the ballroom who recorded the show. Norris doubted there was anything that transpired at the show that affected the performer's doomed flight, but he was determined to be diligent. It was possible there could be a clue there. Young Mr. Robertson remembered the name.

Norris pondered other implications of the recording. Although he wasn't for sure if the recording was illegal or not, he did find it highly unusual. If it was illegal, he certainly didn't have time to get caught up in another issue *and* deal with the investigation on the ground as well.

Figuring it would serve him better to gather as much assistance as he could in the high profile case, Norris put a call in to the Federal Communications Commission.

DANNY WHITE

10:00 A.M., FCC HEADQUARTERS, WASHINGTON, D.C.

FCC Headquarters." The switchboard operator announced impersonally.

"Hello, Inspector Andrew Norris with the CAB here. May I speak to Director Heinrich Marlowe, please?"

"Yes, certainly, but you have the wrong office. He's the Director of Broadcast Security. That division is no longer a part of our office. I'll patch you over."

The phone rang twice. In a dark Washington office, a portly, somewhat unkempt man in suspenders took a drag from his cigar and finished his Bloody Mary. He reached for the phone and acknowledged the call.

"Marlowe speaking." A new gold lighter, being twirled incessantly between the director's thumb and index finger, preoccupied his thoughts.

"Director Marlowe," answered Norris, too brightly, nervous, "Andrew Norris with the Civil Aeronautics Board. How are you this morning?"

"Fine," he offered the curt response, somewhat more attentive. "For what or whom might I owe the pleasure of talking to the CAB this morning?"

Norris could practically smell Marlowe's pungent, cigar smoke and Vodka tainted breath coming through the receiver."

"Director, we're in Iowa investigating the crash that killed some performers here early yesterday morning. Have you heard the reports about the accident involving Buddy Holly and a few fellow musicians?"

"Yes. Yes I have. It's too bad." The director answered, unmoved. "Well known guys, I believe? Hmmm, terrible thing it is." The director didn't appear too discomforted by the news.

"Yes, well——"

"What can I do for you, inspector?" The director's tone impelled Norris to speak quickly.

Explaining the issue with the tapes, the recording of the show, and how they might possibly help the investigation in finding some clues, Agent Norris asked for Marlowe's help. The line crackled in silence for a moment. The director's voice came back, after a long hesitation, booming with assurance and good will.

"Indeed, I believe we can help Inspector Norris. The OBS will get to the bottom of it and secure those tapes. We'll find them, take a listen and let you know."

Relieved of the workload, Norris responded gratefully. "Thank you. Do you have a notion of when your man will be arriving?"

Marlowe assured him. "As a matter of fact we have someone in the area already. I'll have him contacted and redirected to you as soon as possible."

"You'll be looking for a young man named Daniels, Billy Daniels from Clear Lake. He has the tapes we're looking for."

"Billy Daniels," Marlowe grunted. "I'll pass it along. Good day."

I'm glad that's over . . . not the nicest man I've ever spoken to. Norris thought, turning to the pyramid of paperwork in front of him. *At least it's off of my shoulders. It's their issue to deal with now.*

10:10 A.M., THE OFFICE OF BROADCAST SECURITY, WASHINGTON, D.C.

Rock 'n' roll music first blipped the FCC's radar screen when Ike Turner and his Kings of Rhythm hit the airwaves with "Rocket 88" in 1951. With its disturbingly loud hypnotic beat, sung by teens cavorting in front of young, screaming fans, rock and roll had become a real concern, especially to certain segments of the American public.

In 1954, Bill Haley's "Rock Around The Clock" transformed rock 'n' roll from a fledgling format into a full-blown phenomenon. Immediately after broadcasts of the song, the FCC would become overrun with calls to ban the music from radio by outraged listeners.

In response, the U.S. Government created the Office of Broadcast Security, a division of the FCC that would wage a fulltime crusade against degenerative music forms such as rock 'n' roll. The directive of the new division was wide reaching. Everything from scanning the airwaves for objectionable content to tracking down rogue radio stations and forcing record labels to play only "acceptable content" was part of the OBS mission. With Marlowe at the helm, the division was known for their hardball approach to banning music that didn't meet certain "guidelines."

As OBS Director, Marlowe inherently thought rock 'n' roll or "black music," was a menace to society. As far as he was concerned, it represented all that was degenerate in America's youth and their disrespect for traditional norms. On the other hand, if there was something in it for him, he was known to be a man that could be persuaded to turn a blind eye, depending on the price.

In 1955, Marlowe was behind a proposal to make a change in the United States copyright laws prohibiting any white singer from performing or recording rhythm and blues cover songs. Taking it a step further later that year, he supported a ban on rock 'n' roll dances, public dancing, or events where "rock and roll dancing might happen," insisting they be banned or monitored in some way by the government.

It was an excellent scheme that increased his importance to the industry while at the same time made breaking a record more costly . . . ensuring some of the record label expense would end up in his pocket.

By 1957 Marlowe began targeting the record labels, or those recording companies that actively sought out and supported certain styles of music. These companies were subtly *and* openly threatened if they didn't comply with his set of "rules." For the labels that went along, their records would magically go to the top of the charts, for those that didn't, radio play was nearly impossible to obtain.

Approved artists were treated lavishly and Director Marlowe saw to it that certain artists and recording companies were afforded opportunities on television, pulling the strings behind the scenes, creating overnight superstars. He proved to the industry that the OBS could make or break cash flow streams in the wink of an eye and enjoyed wielding the power whenever he needed to. As a show of power, Marlowe and his enforcer, Agent Karl Stoneman leaned hard on the producers of *The Ed Sullivan Show*, preventing Elvis Presley from being filmed below the waist during his September 9, 1957 appearance. It turned out to be the coup de' grace of censorship.

By censuring the most popular rock 'n' roll singer in the business, on the highest rated television show in the country, Marlowe made his point loud and clear, leaving no doubt about who was in charge of the music business. It had nothing to do with "hip swinging" and everything to do with who had the deepest pockets.

By 1959, Marlowe had amassed a small fortune by turning a blind eye toward certain music that the OBS could have banned. All expense paid vacations to Las Vegas and Florida showed up regularly in the mailbox of his home. Gold watches, wads of cash, and boxes of Cuban cigars suddenly appeared around Christmas time from grateful record executives to whom he had shown favoritism.

Upon learning of the tapes made in Clear Lake, Marlowe quickly surmised the opportunity. *The Winter Dance Party* tapes, if in his possession, presented a tremendous advantage. If they turned out to be as they were reported, he would be in full control of their release, and at a price of his choosing. There was in the tapes, a king's ransom to be made.

The director was not misleading the CAB investigator in regard to his Agent. Karl Stoneman was already in the Midwest, keeping an eye on *The Winter Dance Party*. His presence on the tour was due to an overwhelming number of complaints about *Chantilly Lace*, a particularly risqué song by J.P. Richardson. His man witnessed Buddy Holly's last performance as well, and, if he was quick enough, he might be able to catch the agent before he left for his next assignment on the west coast.

THE LAST ROCK AND ROLL SHOW

10:15 A.M., THE COMSTOCK HOTEL, MOORHEAD, MINNESOTA

OBS Agent Karl Stoneman was a company man, spending the last two decades in one agency or the other, chasing down anyone the federal government asked him to go after. Until recently, Stoneman relished the role of hatchet man for the higher-ups; mercilessly bringing the law down on people and making them suffer. It was his specialty and what he was known for, but his rank was starting to wear thin. He lived and survived in the business by keeping the old adage, "Keep your friends close and your enemies closer." However, as of late, he was becoming more interested in eliminating his enemies.

That same adage was precisely the reason Marlow wanted him around. If he could keep his eye on Stoneman, and his executioner style tactics, it meant he wouldn't be coming after him. In organizations like the OBS, they tended to eat their own and Marlowe knew the tactics better than anyone in the business.

Still, Marlowe who was consumed with power possessed very few personal relationship skills and enjoyed treating Stoneman like a doormat. The Agent had packed his luggage and was ready to head toward warmer surroundings when the phone rang.

The director barked. "What's going on, and what are you doing?"

"Just finished my report sir, looking forward to getting out of here and on to Califor—"

"Los Angeles will have to wait," his boss said swiftly, cutting him off.

"I need you to go back to Iowa."

"Iowa? Why do I need to go back to Iowa?" Stoneman blurted.

"I want you to find a kid named Billy Daniels." The director answered, clearly annoyed at being questioned. "The CAB called today looking for some interviews the Daniels boy taped with Buddy Holly on Monday night. They're looking for clues in regard to the crash and think there may be some information on the tapes. You know about the crash, right?"

"Of course I know about it," Stoneman answered, with no trace of compassion or care in his voice. "That's what you get when you fly in a snow storm."

"You *were* at the venue in Clear Lake weren't you?" The director needled, aware of Stoneman's growing irritation.

"Yes, of course I was." Stoneman shot back. An indignant tone colored his voice.

"Then how in the hell did you miss someone carrying around a tape recorder? Since you were there, you should have no problem recognizing who we're looking for. That is if you were paying any attention."

"Sir, I—"

"Find Daniels, confiscate those tapes, and bring them to Washington." The director demanded, his voice thick with unrestrained anger. Do you understand me?"

"Yes sir, I—"

There was suddenly a dial tone at the other end of the line.

Blind rage flew through Stoneman's veins, cursing his rank and vowing to change his position on "the ladder" of the OBS. He blasted to only the walls of his cold room. *I'm out here screwing around on this two bit rock and roll tour in the frozen tundra when the real prize is in Los Angeles!*

The investigation he was finishing up on the west coast could catapult him into a major promotion if he was successful. If that promotion happened, it would make going on miserable assignments like the current one he had to endure, a long gone memory.

After checking out of the hotel, Stoneman began searching for flights to Clear Lake, but it wasn't looking good. The weather was whipping up a dagger like torrent and the only option was a small plane. A 4:00 p.m. flight was as good as he could do.

Small planes, he thought to himself, dragging his suitcase to the curb of the frozen street. *I hate this crap, spending my life running around these hill jack towns for that lousy excuse of a paycheck they give me. I'm going to make this Daniels boy miserable. I should be having a drink at the Formosa tonight. Instead, I've got to drag myself back to that God-forsaken ice box.*

10
11:59 A.M., THE EL RANCHO HOTEL, GALLUP, NEW MEXICO

It was turning out to be another slow morning for Rosetta Aspinall, the new part-time hostess at the El Rancho Hotel. The elegant woman with flowing auburn hair and deep green eyes had been on the job for less than six months and still hadn't quite adjusted to the new pace. Accustomed to her mile-a-minute life in California as part of the Hollywood film industry, living in Gallup was proving to be quite a change. The speed of a small town and living with her parents presented a challenge to get accustomed to, but she was making it work.

Her impeccable British accent and striking appearance was a little out of place at the El Rancho but the guests loved her, adding yet another exotic flavor to the storied Hotel. Rose, as her friends called her, didn't need the money offered by the El Rancho position, but she did need the break. The decision to leave Hollywood to help her family, proved to be an easy one to make. Her father was seriously ill and her mother needed help as caregiver for her husband. She was well aware that careers are important, but careers come and go. You only get one Dad.

She was thankful for the time she got to spend with her parents but equally thankful for the job that allowed her to take her mind off of the situation at home. The strain of taking care of her father, especially knowing the outcome of his illness was inevitable, drained her energies as no movie production schedule had before.

The El Rancho was a familiar surrounding for Rose, and in many ways it felt like a home away from home. She had planned the party for her parent's thirtieth wedding anniversary in the hotel's fabulous lobby and for years she enjoyed attending parties at the El Rancho when she was home during Thanksgiving. The El Rancho had long been a lodging provider for company personnel when on location shoots in the desert and many memorable movie moments were shared at the motel, widely known for its association with stars of the silver screen.

Rose loved New Mexico, but was born half a world away in Lancashire, England in 1923. She and her family arrived in America during troubled times brought about by World War II.

Her father, Dr. John Aspinall was a Professor of Science at Oxford University when the British were forced to declare war on Germany in September of 1939. Soon after, he was called to serve his country.

With war on their heels, her father, a respected physicist working secretly as a simple math professor at Oxford, was moved from their home in Lancashire to Bletchley Park in Milton Keynes. Bletchley was primarily known for its Nazi code breaking work in the war, but few knew it was also the home for research of an even greater significance.

At Oxford University, Dr. Aspinall was known for his boring, workman-like approach to mathematics. However, in his private hours, he was quite different, spending hours upon end in closed chambers, running experiments, testing and retesting mathematical formulas, searching for answers to cosmic mysteries within the infinitesimal innards of the hydrogen atom. Dr. Aspinall was one of many university professors across England that led double lives, teaching innocuously during the day, and researching deadly weapons at night. The hand of Adolf Hitler forced the research to a new, and urgent level.

In the spring of 1940, the war was going badly for the British. By June, after a crushing defeat at Dunkirk, Britain's nuclear development program was abandoned. From that point on, all efforts were focused on the defense of the home islands and a possible land invasion by Germany. Later that month, the United States Department of Defense called Number 10 Downing Street, the office of the British Prime Minister, asking for help in regard to solving the "nuclear problem." Aspinall's name was continually mentioned in Washington meetings, as someone that could help in unraveling the issue. Shortly thereafter, with the blessing of King George VI, a deal was struck to put him on loan to the United States . . . more valuable working with the Americans on nuclear fission than ducking bombs in England.

On June 29, the Aspinall's with 17 year-old Rosetta in tow, boarded a Douglas DC-3 bound for the Lakehurst Naval Air Station in New Jersey. Soon they travelled by private Pullman passenger car for the seven day train trip to their new home, Los Alamos, New Mexico.

After the attack on Pearl Harbor the next year, Aspinall and his team were re-stationed to a new facility and Rose left for Southern California. Family friends offered Rose, now no longer a minor, a position in their film supply business after learning that she would not be allowed to follow her family to the new, top secret research facility.

Los Angeles sounded exciting to Rose. Although she would miss her parents, she looked forward to the job. With the war on there would be plenty of work creating war films and support reels for the troops as well as updates from the front. It seemed like only yesterday . . .

"It's been a great place to stay," Michael said, handing over his room key, looking again at the soft walls, thickly coated in cool southwest stucco. The solid, oft-polished oak counter top of the front desk warmly reflected the morning sun as Rose returned the key to its appropriate hook on the wall. A smile appeared on her face.

"I'm glad you enjoyed yourself Mr. Minton." Rose's cultured, British accent evoked images of a faraway land as he took the receipt for his room.

"I've always wanted to visit," he blurted out, wanting to strike up a conversation with his host in hopes of learning more about the place. "My mother spent a couple of days here a long time ago and told me about its history."

"The Hotel has certainly participated in its share of glitz and glamour," Rose added, her bright green eyes warm, fathomless pools of jade. She offered her hand. "My name is Rosetta, but my friends call me Rose. Where are you off to this morning?"

Michael hesitated. "Hollywood, California," he finally answered, taking her hand, "you can call me Michael."

"Well that's my town you're going to visit!" She answered, the burr of her accent taking on added warmth. "What takes you to Hollywood?"

"It's been my life's dream to be an actor," he stuttered, "now I'm finally taking the chance."

"Before you leave, let me show you around," Rose offered kindly, noting his avid interest in the movie stars' photos liberally posted along the walls.

Michael drank it all in as Rose walked him through the old wooden halls with heavy oaken doors decorated by ornate wrought iron hardware. She freely shared stories with Michael about the movies the hotel had been a part of. Ronald Reagan, Kirk Douglas, Spencer Tracy, Katherine Hepburn. All of these stars, at one time or another called the El Rancho home over the prior two decades.

Rose handed him the hotel's business card as they arrived back at the lobby, ending the tour. "Take one of these with you. If I can be of any help when you get to California, give me a ring."

Michael smiled at her. "It's more than kind of you. I appreciate it very much. Thank you Rose."

He tucked the black and white card in his pocket, turned to wave, and was on his way again. California was waiting.

Rose saluted him with the age-old theatrical wish for luck as he walked out the door, "Break a Leg!"

He was going to need it.

5:00 P.M., ROUTE 66, ALBUQUERQUE, NEW MEXICO

In the Fairlane, Annie took on the duties of scout, looking for any signs of a hotel on a ranch or anything close to that description. She picked up postcards and scanned the billboards, keeping her eyes peeled for any clue along the highway. The little sleuth perused every pit stop along the way, scavenging advertisements and promotional flyers until the glut of materials covered the entirety of the backseat, spilling onto the floorboards.

The searchers hoped to find something in the panhandle of Texas as everyone agreed there should be a ranch or twenty in the area. When they got to Amarillo, they gave the "Cattle Capital of the West," a good look over, but the whole town *was* a ranch. An hour was lost just trying to find a parking place. Semi trucks hauling cattle from the nation's livestock crossroads covered the dusty town like a diesel fueled blanket.

A little further down the road, there was the Ranch House in Tucumcari, New Mexico. After seeing the name on a billboard, they sped into the parking lot, eyes wide open, only to find a small, stand alone cafe.

There wasn't a clue to be found about the mysterious hotel. Instead, they found only dusty brown hills and bleached white rock for miles. The New Mexico state line passed under their wheels and tension grew inside the Fairlane. That tension began to feel like it could be cut with the scissors Annie was using to hack up the advertisements she was collecting. They needed to turn up something soon. Billy's stomach began that same, slow, uneasy churning again.

As they rolled down Central Avenue in Albuquerque, the road-weary threesome decided they needed to take a break and parked the car on the main drag. Just before sundown, the neon menagerie of Albuquerque's famous boulevard began sparkling to life. Their legs needed a stretch, and their minds a break from the non-stop gumshoeing for the Cadillac.

The town was abuzz as they walked past the impressive Art Deco Kimo Theater, ablaze in lights and spilling over with eager movie goers. They strolled through a western shop offering hand tooled leather boots and saddles, then crossed the street to a Curio shop selling Indian goods.

Maisel's Indian and Curio's shop carried nearly every kind of souvenir that anyone could possibly want. Everything from dream catchers to traditional pottery and turquoise encrusted silver jewelry could be purchased at Maisel's. Like all of the other souvenir shops along Route 66, there were racks of advertisements and brochures. Annie of course, picked every one of them clean.

"I'm starved, let's go get some grub." Billy suggested impatiently, more than slightly embarrassed by his sister's obscene haul of advertisements from the store.

Maisel's clerk craned his head in their direction, nodding as he made a "shooing away" gesture with his hand, realizing the tire kickers weren't going to buy anything.

Ducking their heads inside the Liberty Cafe, the restaurant looked like the ideal place to have a little "comfort" food. Before dinner arrived, Annie plopped the cache' of information on the table in front of them. It needed attention.

She began, droning out lodging titles. "Glenrio Hotel, Josey Joe's 66 Shady Stop, Uranium City–"

The waitress arrived at their table, wearing a robin's egg blue uniform with a white, food stained apron. She was obviously having a very long day.

"We've still got fried chicken, okra, mashed potatoes, and green beans. What'll ya have?"

"We'll take three plates of 'em." Billy said politely.

"Can I have my plate with none of the vegetables touching each other please?" Annie smiled, hoping the waitress was paying attention, then, picked up where she left off.

"Lux Movie Theater Discount, Cline's Corners, See the Continental Divide, Before Man Walked the Earth-Visit the Petrified Forest, Painted Desert–"

"Can we stop for a little while?" DJ interrupted, irritated and reaching for his caffeine fix. "I can't listen to any more of it right now."

They were starting to crack. On the road non-stop for over thirty hours, and sleeping in the car was starting to catch up with them. Billy felt the same way and couldn't fault DJ for being frustrated. Annie on the other hand, looked completely unflappable as the straw in her Orange Crush soda pop made an annoying slurping sound.

The waitress returned, balancing a full tray of food on one hand with the skill of long experience. "Three fried chickens with veggies coming your way,"

Billy thought aimlessly while the waitress set the plates on the table, looking for an answer.

Everybody knows everybody else in a small town . . . maybe a bigger one too.

"Excuse me ma'am." He called to the waitress, already making her way back to the kitchen. She turned.

"Did I leave ya short?"

"No, not at all," he assured her, "just wanted to know if you've lived around here long."

"My whole life unfortunately," she reached up to fix a loose hair pin, huffed, then winked at Billy, "still waitin' for Prince Charming to come and sweep me away."

Billy cleared his throat, and squirmed a bit. "I hate to trouble you, but we're having an awful time. We're trying to find a hotel that's on a ranch or maybe has ranch in its name. Any place around here like that ring a bell?"

The waitress looked at him oddly, chewing her gum open mouthed. "Not really."

Billy decided to press a little further before he turned to the plate full of chicken.

"Supposed to be a place where movie stars stay, or has some sort of film connection?"

"Oh yeah!" The waitress's face brightened and the gum chomping stopped momentarily. "I thought you meant here in Albuquerque! You're talking about the El Rancho Hotel in Gallup. Everybody knows about that place. It's about two hours from here."

DJ nearly choked on his coffee, spewing it all over the table.

Annie's slurping stopped, and a wide smile formed across Billy's face.

The waitress perked up, temporarily startled by the reaction. Then, the chomping began again in earnest. "I assume this means I'm going to get a big tip...or maybe I've found my Prince!"

DANNY WHITE

9:30 P.M., THE EL RANCHO HOTEL, GALLUP, NEW MEXICO

The sun had slipped off beyond the horizon hours earlier as DJ turned the Fairlane into the parking lot of the El Rancho Hotel. Quickly they began searching for the Cadillac, hoping to find Michael somewhere nearby.

"Nothing," DJ cursed briefly.

"It was just too much time to make up," Billy offered as consolation. "Let's go inside and see if we can find anything."

The trio walked into the hotel lobby and began to wander toward the front desk. A voice came lightly from behind.

"Welcome to the El Rancho. May I help you?"

"Yes ma'am, thank you." He decided that throwing a Hail Mary couldn't hurt. "Have you seen a guy about our age in a new Cadillac around here today?"

Rose looked at him with infinite coolness, then, motioned to the low, cowhide covered couches arranged comfortably by the fire in the middle of the lobby.

"I've seen plenty of young people here today. Please, have a seat."

Rose and the three travelers sat down on the knotty pine framed couches, with plush down pillows arranged at each corner. It was a welcome change from the confines of the Fairlane.

"I don't usually pay attention to what kind of motorcars our guests are driving. Although we do require that our guests provide pertinent information about their vehicle on the hotel registration card." She raised her eyebrows and prompted, "Do you have a name for the person you're looking for?"

"Yes, Ma'am. Yes we do." Billy's replied. "His name is Michael. Michael Minton."

Rose looked to her lap, smoothing her navy blue dress over her knees, responding slowly with caution.

"He stayed with us last night and left around 1:00 p.m. this afternoon. He said he was going to my old home town, Hollywood. He's a very nice young man. Are you friends of his?"

"Yes, well . . . yes we are." Billy stumbled, trying to gain his footing and figure out an approach. "We're trying to contact him."

Annie blurted out, "Would it be too much trouble if we were to look at his registration card?"

DJ added with a rush, "It's really important."

"No trouble at all," she nodded, leading them toward the front desk. "Let's go look it up."

Filing through the registrations, she plucked the three-by-five index card from a small wooden box sitting on the counter.

"Here it is," she said laying the card on the desk between them, "Number Three: The Alan Ladd Room." Billy's index finger traced each entry on the card.

DANNY WHITE

```
Name: Michael Minton
Vehicle Make: Cadillac
Color: Green
License Plate number: XD4900
```

Looking up from the card with a grimace, Billy held out his hand. "My name is Billy Daniels. This is my best friend DJ and my little sister Annie."

Rose responded not yet knowing what to make of the inquiry. "My name is Rosetta Aspinall it's a pleasure to meet you."

"Miss Aspinall, do you have a few minutes to talk to us?" Worry pinched Billy's forehead. "We have a little problem."

A few minutes turned into two hours. After being told of the events leading up to their meeting, Rose convinced the young travelers that staying the night was the best idea. There was no way to catch up to Michael in her estimation and stated that he was probably only a few hours from Los Angeles anyway. Soon, Michael would be melded into the bowels of the city and finding him would be next to impossible for anyone not familiar with Los Angeles.

Rose made them feel at home at the El Rancho. The hotel seemed an oasis in a rolling sea of uncertainty that only offered one mirage after another. After the thirty-two hour trek to Gallup, it was time to temporarily stop the chase. Initially, Billy wanted to leave earlier and chafed at the decision to stay. Finally, he admitted to himself that they didn't have a chance of catching Michael, especially given that it was already so late and approaching morning. If they stayed, the possibility remained that maybe, just maybe, Rose could help.

★★★★★★★★★★★★★★★★★★★★★★★★★

FEBRUARY 5, 1959
CORRUPTION AND CALIFORNIA

★★★★★★★★★★★★★★★★★★★★★★★★★

11
6:00 A.M., ROUTE 66, GALLUP, NEW MEXICO

Rose turned out to be a godsend, staying up with them until midnight, working out options and giving them an insider's look at Los Angeles. Rose knew nearly everyone in Hollywood it seemed, and suggested a place for them to stay during their search.

It was more than they could have hoped for after a string of bad breaks. Rose gave them a reason to carry on, confirming that Michael said he was in fact headed for Hollywood. Their inability to catch Michael the night before turned out to be a blessing in disguise.

Rose handed Billy a piece of El Rancho letterhead. "It's about 13 hours from here to the Santa Monica Pier if you stay on Route 66. This is the name of the hotel I've reserved for you and my friend's phone number. Call her when you get there."

Billy scanned the note, written in Rose's professional script.

The Roosevelt Hotel, Hollywood.
Jill Lovelle
828 Linda Flora Way
Bel Air, California
Tele: BElair 5-2740

He stuck the piece of paper in his pocket and asked if he could make a quick phone call. He needed to report in.

"Mr. Minton?"

"Yes, Billy!" Fred's anxious voice rose hopefully. "Where are you son?"

"We found the motel, it's called The El Rancho and it's in New Mexico. We're getting ready to leave for California, I wanted to call to let you know we're alright."

"Good, I've been worried sick. "Do you know if Michael is okay?"

"He was here at the hotel, and we're told that he's fine." Billy continued. "You were right . . . he's going to tinsel town."

Billy filled him in on the rest of the details, leaving the name of the hotel where they could be reached in Hollywood.

"Is there anything I can do here?" Fred asked, sticking the information to the tackboard above his desk.

"We're doing fine. Billy answered. "We'll give it until Saturday night. If we can't find him, we'll just come on home and face the firing sqaud."

"You've already gone a long way Billy." Fred interjected, trying to find something light hearted to say. "You might as well get to see the ocean for your trouble."

DANNY WHITE

8:05 A.M., MINTON TOWING COMPANY, CLEAR LAKE, IOWA

Fred hung up the phone and went back to digging out from under the backlog of work piled up since the storm.

"Hey, Boss!" Eddie hollered as he lumbered through the front door. "You look like a brand new man this morning."

"Thanks, I feel better than I have all week," he said, returning a fragile salute, "just got off the phone with Billy a few minutes ago."

"Michael?" The question arched on Eddie's bushy eyebrows.

"They didn't find him but he's alright." A hint of a smile formed on Fred's face, "that's something to be thankful for today."

"You deserve a little good news," said Eddie, "it's been a long time coming."

Fred turned his mind to the day's business, nodding at the car hanging on the hook of Wrecker #1. He cast a look in Eddie's direction.

"I've got to get this Edsel over to Des Moines . . . watch the shop for me?"

"Sure." Eddie replied, as if there would be any doubt.

Fred jumped into the cab of the huge truck. "I'll be gone most of the day . . . still a bunch of snow over in the big city and more on the way."

Eddie yelled as Fred took off. "Take yer time and don't worry about a thing."

THE LAST ROCK AND ROLL SHOW

8:10 A.M., THE CORNER DRUG PAYPHONE, CLEAR LAKE, IOWA

Karl Stoneman got off to an early start in Clear Lake, politely asking around town about Daniels, carefully concealing the details of the investigation. "Routine business," he intoned mechanically to the curious. He had already been to the Daniels residence, finding no one at home. School was closed and the locals had little knowledge of his whereabouts. Asking at the dime store, the bank, and gas station produced the same results. The young recording buff was nowhere to be found. The weather was getting worse, and although it seemed impossible, it was getting colder as well.

Stoneman's cheap leather soles slipped frequently on the frozen sidewalks. The rock salt spread around haphazardly was no match for the brutal elements. He cursed again at the wretch who caused his return.

It's time to call the CAB . . . maybe they've got something. He muttered to himself, reaching for the icy telephone, closing the phone booth door with a snap.

"Operator, give me FLeetwood 7-2161." Stoneman snarled into the mouthpiece, bending toward the receiver in an attempt to block out the street noise.

Inspector Norris answered pleasantly, encouraged by the OBS's swift action. Norris began to recount the information he gathered from the will call list at The Surf.

"One of them was a girl named Mary Lou Evans–

"OK, yeah." Stoneman broke in, "I ain't interested in your blow-by-blow chit-chat with the hoodlums around here, see? Did you get a lead or not?"

Norris stuttered, and continued in a rush. "The Evans girl stated that she met up with her brother and Daniels at the Surf Ballroom, said the two were best friends."

Stoneman pressed coldly. "Did she say anything about where they might be?"

"No. The last time she spoke with him was on Tuesday morning, said he just returned from a towing yard nearby."

Stoneman continued to hammer Norris. "Did she give you a reason?"

"Just said her brother went to help out Daniels and assumed it was to pick up his car. Apparently the boy's vehicle is notorious for draining batteries. That's all we have."

"A towing company you say?" Stoneman asked again.

"Yes, but we didn't get a name."

Stoneman hung up the phone, cutting off Norris' goodbye. He pulled at the phone book dangling from its frosty cable, stomping his numb feet on the ground to start some circulation.

The secretary at Trinkle's answered, saying she hadn't seen anyone fitting the description, and there was no answer at Minton's. A short drive later, Stoneman was knocking at Fred Minton's door.

THE LAST ROCK AND ROLL SHOW

8:25 A.M., MINTON TOWING COMPANY
CLEAR LAKE, IOWA

Federal Agent Stoneman," the hard-nose enforcer spat, holding his badge against a small window in the door.

"Wha . . . what is it?" Eddie mouthed, caught by surprise. He recovered gamely and moved to open the door.

"Come on in out of the cold."

"Is the owner here?" Stoneman said pointedly, wasting no time.

"He's in Des Moines, gonna be gone most of the day. Is there something I can do for ya?"

"Possibly," Stoneman gave an icy reply. "I'm looking for a Billy Daniels and one Darrell Evans. Have you seen them?"

Hesitating for a moment, then, looking back at the Agent, Eddie fumbled with his reply.

"Well, uh, not today."

Stoneman said nothing, waiting, staring malevolently. "Let me put it this way, Mister . . . what was your name?"

"Eddie, Eddie Neal," He babbled, increasingly nervous.

"Mr. Neal," the agent glowered, "have you seen Mr. Daniels or Mr. Evans this week?"

Eddie saw the look on the agent's face. His tone was as serious as a heart attack.

"Yes, I have," he admitted, "they've gone to Los Angeles to get a Cadillac. What's this all about?"

"It's about a set of tapes they have," Stoneman said bluntly. "We need the tapes for the federal investigation into the accident that killed Buddy Holly and his pals. What Cadillac?"

Eddie shifted nervously, nearly stumbling over a set of box end wrenches lying on the shop floor.

"And why would they drive all the way to Los Angeles for a car? Are they picking it up for the company?"

Despite the cold, Eddie's broad face was beaded in sweat.

"Well, umm. I don't—

Stoneman ripped into the burley truck driver, sensing he was trying to hide something.

"Listen to me and listen to me good. I'm only going to say it once." He whipped his polished silver badge back out of a pocket in his full length black leather trench coat. "Lying to a federal agent is a felony offense. You understand me?"

Eddie glanced quickly again at the agent's badge, then spilled the beans on the whole bizarre set of circumstances. He told the Agent about the stolen car, the recordings of the Winter Dance Party, and that Michael had taken the car not knowing the tapes were in the trunk.

Feeling he betrayed his loyalty to Fred by giving the details of Michael's desertion, Eddie hung his head low, staring at the floor.

Stoneman looked dour, rubbing his stiff fingers together. "You gotta phone . . . and a match?"

Eddie gingerly led him to the office and offered him a chair. While he escaped to the supply room for matches, Stoneman reached for his cigarettes and stopped,then squited at the large note pinned to the tack board.

Eddie returned with a greasy pack of matches, but the Agent suddenly rose and exited the shop without saying a word, leaving only his card on Fred's desk.

Stoneman was surprised by the events that Eddie Neal explained to him. It wasn't what he was expecting at all.

Drive all the way to LA for a car? What the hell are these guys thinking? Let the thief go to jail like he should for stealing the —wait a minute . . . the tapes!

The tapes were another story entirely. He struck a match and held it close, lighting the cigarette with half-closed eyes, thinking.

They were recordings of the entire show, not interviews . . . the final show of rock 'n' roll superstars! Smoking by his car, Marlowe's vision and motives came into crystal-clear focus.

I should have seen this one coming. Stoneman thought ruefully, well aware of his boss' profiteering inclinations, and his own whenever he could get away with it.

Realizing the whole charade wasn't about helping the CAB with the investigation, he clapped his hands together in mock applause. He couldn't stand the man, but he had to give it to Marlowe. The old geezer never missed a trick.

Armed with new insight into the game, Stoneman turned out of Minton's parking lot and sped toward the Mason City airport. He would find the tapes, but had no intention of giving them to Director Marlowe.

10:45 A. M.,
METEOR CRATER, ARIZONA

For Pete's sake, will ya go reason with her?" DJ pleaded, lying flat on the hood of the Fairlane, staring into the Arizona sky as Roy Orbison and The Teen Kings, *Go-Go-Go,* pounded out of DJ's radio. The music slapped back in long echoes as it careened off of the massive crater.

The Crater visit had been a relatively routine stop, that was until Annie wandered off, becoming glued to a telescope perched on the edge of the giant, fifty-thousand year old chasm.

"It's no use, she's got a head as hard as the meteor that made that hole." Billy resigned himself to the situation, nodding in the direction of the giant crater. "It's her way or the highway sometimes. You know that."

"Let me guess," DJ said sarcastically. "Right now, it's her way cause we sure as heck ain't on the highway?"

"She's crazy for the stars and planet stuff. I'll do what I can do to get her going, but I'm not promising anything."

Billy understood DJ's frustration. There was enough to go around for everybody. The fact was however that Annie agreed to come along and try to help the best she could. If she had refused, they would still be in Iowa. Moreover, Billy was protective of his little sister, who for all of her smarts was still a fragile, 65-pound kid soaking wet. She could make life difficult for him, but he put up with it. That's what big brothers do.

The gang cleaned out the floorboard and the back seat of the Fairlane when they left Gallup, and the car was spotless. It only lasted a few hours before returning to something similar in scope to the Cerro Gordo County landfill again, after Annie started "collecting" things.

Annie knew that the Painted Desert and Petrified Forest were along the route and had no intention of passing up any of it, stolen Cadillac or not. Painted Indian souvenirs and petrified wood was everywhere. Hanging from the rear window frame; rattle snake tails and strings of mementos she picked up at the gift shops clanked and rattled like muted wind chimes.

Soon there would be high desert dirt in plastic bags labeled "Galaxy Dust," and an assortment of moon rocks from outer space, or closer to the truth; painted gravel from a local side road.

"How about it Annie?" Billy shouted the thinly veiled request to get her back on the road. "We've got a Cadillac to catch."

She pulled slowly away from the telescope, jumping from its viewing platform and arched an eyebrow toward Billy.

"Come with me to the souvenir shop. I need some books for the road."

Billy breathed a sigh of relief, loping swiftly up the path with the little astronomer in tow. Brother and sister bellied up to the gift counter and laid their money down like every other tourist who had come before them paying homage to the crater. They carried the whole lot of her score, back to the Fairlane.

"You've got enough ammunition for a full-on science project in the backseat little lady." DJ hoped to coax her into a complete immersion in the junk so they wouldn't have to stop again for a while.

Peering over the top of her newest book, *"Exploring the Rings of Saturn,"* she answered; "we'll see about that."

DJ turned the Fairlane back onto Route 66 with leaflets occasionally fluttering through the back window and onto the highway as they sped toward Los Angeles.

The Santa Fe Railway's *Super Chief* Luxury Streamliner, blazed across the Arizona desert, speeding toward California side-by-side with the Fairlane. The giant train escorted them out of Arizona, on a straight line due west toward the Pacific Ocean.

THE LAST ROCK AND ROLL SHOW

8:00 P.M., SANTA MONICA PIER, LOS ANGELES, CALIFORNIA

The scenery was breathtaking from Gallup to the Santa Monica Pier, where Route 66 dead ends into a long, sandy beach.

Weaving through the cliff dwellings of Canyon Diablo into the land of the Grand Canyon, DJ put the Fairlane into high gear. From Barstow and Victorville to the Sierra Madre, the foreign landscape of California kept them wide awake. They thrilled at the rugged, sometimes desolate beauty of the West, so different from the pancake flatness of Iowa they were accustomed to.

The Pacific Ocean, dark and seemingly endless, stood in stark contrast to the bright lights and festive atmosphere surrounding the revelers, abuzz around the pier. People waited with snow cones topped with candy syrup, inching in line toward the multi-colored cars of the giant Ferris wheel. Its incandescent bulbs strung along the spokes, humming with electricity while the nearby roller coaster, clickity clacked in time to the shrieks of its riders. The musical menagerie playing in the background, sprinkled with calliopes and accordions, felt like a mid-western county fair, as the gilded sleighs of the carousel whirled by in the salty air.

The trio had been on the pier for about twenty minutes when they returned to the Fairlane, munching on corn dogs and sipping soda pop. Billy was lying on the hood of the car when the most beautiful girl he ever set eyes on, pulled up beside of them in a salmon pink MG convertible. Billy was caught, mesmerized. He couldn't help staring at the young woman with long flowing brown hair, her bright blue eyes sparkling with the reflection of the

Lipizzaner Stallions prancing on the carousel.

She gracefully climbed from the MG and approached them. Billy crammed the rest of his corn dog into a napkin and jumped off of the car about the time she got close enough to stick out her hand.

A smile appeared. "Hello, I'm Jill Lovelle. You must be Billy?"

He recognized her voice immediately as the person he called an hour earlier to come and meet them.

"Yes, hello," he reached for her firm, tanned hand, "I'm Billy. This is my little sister Annie and my best friend DJ."

"Shall we go down to The Roosevelt and get you checked in then?"

DJ stuttered, "Uh . . . yes," his eyes had a glazed over, deer caught in the headlights look.

"Can I ride with you Jill?" Annie asked petulantly. "I don't think these boys will mind."

Jill answered, looking at Billy with the question on her lips. "Of course . . . as long as it's ok with your brother?"

* *

FEBRUARY 6, 1959
TELESCOPES AND DRIVE IN MOVIES

* *

12
4:00 P.M., MINNEAPOLIS-ST. PAUL INTERNATIONAL AIRPORT, MINNESOTA

Karl Stoneman had endured a very long day, even before he reached Minneapolis. Minneapolis-St. Paul was the only airport with a flight to the Los Angeles area. It was cold, crowded, and Stoneman was in a foul mood.

Given the weather conditions, the lay over for the flight to Burbank, California did nothing for his attitude. Cursing the inconvenience, he made his way through the construction of the new Lindbergh Terminal. Stomping every step of the way, the agitated government Rottweiler stormed toward the gate.

An 8 p.m. arrival time might work. He calculated swiftly, as he squeezed through the cabin door of the United DC-7, looking for his seat. *The Roosevelt isn't too far from Burbank.*

Eddie Neal had indeed been helpful, although for the most part, unknowingly. More than the information that Stoneman squeezed out of Neal, the note from the tack board at Minton's proved to be the best score of all. The Agent lifted it from underneath the single, chrome thumb tack, like a seasoned criminal.

It'll be like taking candy from a baby. He smiled unpleasantly, fastening his seat belt. *Find out where these tapes are, and then focus on the Big Kahuna.*

It was time to bring the hammer down on the investigation that took him over a year to complete. The high profile seizure would be the crowning achievement of his career.

6:00 P.M.,
LOS ANGELES, CALIFORNIA

Michael spent the whole day out looking for work although it felt more like he was just getting good at asking directions, than actually finding employment. The day garnered few leads, not great but not bad for his first day of hoofing it around LA. The only promising morsel he was able to round up related to a casting opportunity the following week. However, finding the cattle call on his street guide of Los Angeles was proving to be difficult at best.

He was just about to give up on finding it when he remembered the business card in his jacket from the El Rancho Hotel.

The phone rang twice. Rose answered sounding pleased to hear from him, and relayed the directions he needed while trying to conceal her emotions about the luck of the call.

"Are you enjoying Los Angeles, Michael?" She asked innocently.

"I'm enjoying it very much, although making my way around town is a bit tough at times!" He admitted.

"The city will be old hat to you before you know it." It just takes a little time. Any plans for this evening?"

"Yeah," he said excitedly. "I'm going to do a little sight seeing. I am in Hollywood after all!"

"Wonderful," she answered in her disarmingly kind voice, "any place special in mind?"

"Yes, as a matter of fact there is. I'm going to visit my favorite '*Rebel Without A Cause*' spot first."

"The Griffith Observatory!" She said knowledgeably. "The mountain offers a wonderful view of the city."

"If I have time I might go to the Victory Drive-In a little later. Hitchcock's *Vertigo* is playing. I've always been a big fan of his movies."

Rose encouraged him. "I just saw *Vertigo* a couple of weeks ago. It's an extraordinary piece of work. I've been to the Victory a few times myself. I even remember when it opened!"

"It sounds like a fun theatre," he guessed. "If I don't make it out there this time, maybe I can do it next week."

"I hope you have a fabulous evening Michael, whatever you decide to do. Call me anytime."

Hanging up the phone after exchanging good byes, she congratulated herself.

THE LAST ROCK AND ROLL SHOW

Maybe I'm the one who should have been the actress!

Rose had known thousands of "Michaels" over the years. Scores of young actors and actresses came into her office, following their dreams and taking their chances with little money and no one to call for guidance.

The odds were stacked against the pilgrims hoping to become movie-house immortals, yet at the same time, some of the greatest came to Hollywood, with nothing more than a shirt on their back and made it big. She knew many of them and considered her self fortunate to call them friends.

Putting the momentary respect for her performance aside, she immediately dialed The Hotel Roosevelt.

The front desk clerk answered and patched her into Room #223.

The phone rang loudly in the empty room.

No answer.

13
7:15 P.M., THE ROOSEVELT HOTEL, HOLLYWOOD, CALIFORNIA

After a fruitless day of searching, Billy, DJ, Jill, and Annie arrived back at the Roosevelt. No one felt good about their chances and they weren't any closer to finding Michael than they were at 8:00 a.m. when they started. The Roosevelt was nice, but Billy wasn't keen on the idea of spending Fred's money on a fancy hotel, even though Rose arranged a discount for them. After Jill invited the Iowan's to her parent's house in Bel Air for the rest of the weekend, they took her up on the offer.

As they collected their things, the bakelite rotary telephone on the nightstand caught Jill's eye. Its red light was blinking.

"There's a message waiting at the front desk," she motioned to Billy as the others filed out of the room toward the elevator, "let's pick it up on our way out."

"May I help you?" The front desk clerk inquired, taking in Billy's pinched, anxious face and rumpled clothing.

"Yes sir." Billy tried to smooth out a crease in his jacket. "I believe I have a phone message waiting. Room 223?"

"Of course, one moment please."

After a short pause, the starched grey suit and gold cuff link adorned desk boss retrieved the message.

"Ah, yes. Mr. Daniels. Mrs. Rose Aspinall left you a message, requesting that you dial her in New Mexico. She states that it is most urgent."

Billy felt his pulse quicken. He bumped into Jill, leaning in closely behind him, listening intently.

"Use the house phone . . . over there." She pointed to the white phone on the wall. Within seconds the phone was ringing in Gallup. Rose's familiar voice answered.

"Hello, El Rancho Hotel. May I help you?"

"Rose. Billy Daniels here. What's happening?"

"Billy!" She sighed with relief. "Thank goodness you've called. I don't know if you're going to have time but it may be your lucky day. I know where Michael is or at least where he's going to be."

Finally a lucky break. Billy thought.

"He called me over an hour ago," she explained hurriedly. "Is Jill there? I need to talk to her please."

Billy put the phone in Jill's hand.

"Yes, right." Jill's face took on a frown of concentration, her brown hair obscuring Billy's view of the exchange. "We have to go there first. It makes sense. OK. The Victory Drive-In, Hitchcock. I've got it, right. We will. Love you too."

Jill hung up the phone and turned quickly to Billy and the group, bending to help Annie with the zipper on her suitcase. "We've got to get out of here right now."

"What did she say?" Billy asked, holding the door open as they piled out into the cool evening air, stuffing what luggage they had in the trunk of the Fairlane.

"We need to get to the Griffith Observatory as fast as we can. Rose said that Michael may be going to the Victory Drive-In but will be at Griffith for sure."

Billy's thoughts whirled. "If we miss him at the Observatory we'll try and catch him at the movie?"

Jill glanced over quickly, winking at him. "Very good Mr. Daniels. We should be able to make it to the Victory well before the movie is over."

Ten minutes later they were speeding down Hollywood Boulevard on the way to Colonel Griffith J. Griffith's contribution to the City of Los Angeles.

THE LAST ROCK AND ROLL SHOW

8:10 P.M., NORTH VERMONT AVE, HOLLYWOOD, CALIFORNIA

DJ sped through the rolling neighborhoods, up Mount Hollywood, passing the Greek Theater, and navigating between the mansions and palm trees lining Vermont Canyon Drive. Chuck Berry's "*Reelin' and Rockin'*" blasted from DJ's radio, nearly ripping his speaker to shreds.

The Fairlane screamed as they slid into the parking lot of 2800 East Observatory Avenue, skidding sideways to a stop.

Jumping out of the car; each dashed for a different corner of the parking lot searching for the Cadillac and then met at the steps of the observatory.

"Nothing." DJ said. "Not a trace."

Annie huffed, completely out of breath. "No sign of Uncle Earl's car on my side."

Billy stood, holding the stitch at his side, looking back at Annie and Jill. "He could have walked up from the lower lot."

Jill nodded, acknowledging the possibility.

"Little sis, you come with me." Billy directed. "Jill, you and DJ split up. Let's cover this place and meet back here."

Scrambling through the sprawling 1930s Art Deco wonder that was the Griffith Observatory, Billy didn't have time to take in the spectacular view that the mountain top perch offered. He was close to finding the tapes, or at least thought he was.

They scanned every nook and cranny of the stargazing complex then charged back to the observatory steps, disheveled and disheartened.

Billy gasped again, his lungs straining for air. "He's gone . . . he's gone already."

DJ shrugged his shoulders, accepting the verdict and agreeing with Billy.

The lights on the massive HOLLYWOOD sign, set into the hills behind them, tripped on as darkness fell across the mountain.

"The first movie starts at the drive-in around sunset. The feature around," Jill glanced at her Tiffany watch showing 9:00 p.m., "around now."

"We'll be able to find him at the movie if he's there." Billy stated, his natural confidence pooling to the surface.

DJ, ready to burn rubber, began pulling the keys to the Fairlane out of his pocket.

"The Victory is about thirty minutes from here." Jill started toward the car, but stopped in her tracks.

Billy, close behind, nearly collided with her as her hair whipped against his chest when she quickly turned around. She looked back at him with panic on her face. "What?" He frowned.

"Where's Annie?"

He stared, puzzled. "She's right behind–"

THE LAST ROCK and ROLL SHOW

9:05 P.M., THE ROOSEVELT HOTEL, HOLLYWOOD, CALIFORNIA

Stoneman vented his frustration at the taxi driver, struggling from the small cab parked in front of the Roosevelt Hotel.

"Here's my tip: Get out of the taxi driving business!"

Grabbing at his suitcase that threatened to fall to the curb, Stoneman complained loudly again, throwing the five-dollar fare at the driver through the open window. "You're the slowest driver in America! Someday someone's gonna run you off the road, and it might be me! I should have been here an hour ago!"

He grumbled, walking to the hotel's front desk. "My name is Agent Karl Stoneman," he snapped, interrupting the desk clerk assisting a hotel patron. "I'm looking for a guest of yours, Billy Daniels. What room is he in? It's official government business."

"Sir," the clerk quickly looked up, momentarily startled by the out-burst, recovering with a pat to the collar of his suit and said formally; "It is our policy at The Hollywood Roosevelt Hotel to keep our guest information private. I'm sorry but I won't be able to give you the information you are requesting. May I help you with something else?"

Stoneman fumed, snatching the OBS badge from his jacket pocket, holding it an inch from the man's face. "If you don't want every police officer for a city block in this lobby in the next ten minutes, you'll tell me what room Daniels is in right now! I know he's here."

Hotel guests standing nearby turned toward the commotion at the front desk, drawing an uneasy smile from the clerk. He reached up, gently pushing the badge away and lifted a hand to interrupt the Agent. His eyes anxiously scanned the gathering crowd.

"One moment please." The clerk walked back into the manager's office, and slowly returned.

"It looks like we will be able to help you after all."

"That's more like it," Stoneman leered.

Scrolling through the registrations, the clerk took his time while Stoneman waited, vibrating with impatience.

"Yes of course, here it is." The clerk drew the registration. "Mr. Billy Daniels from Iowa. He *was* in Room #223."

"What do you mean he *was?*"

Every ounce of blood in the agent's body seemed to be rushing to his face.

"What I mean by *was*, is that he *was* here." The clerk straightened his glasses and gave Stoneman a broad smile. "That is until about an hour ago, when he checked out."

9:30 P.M., THE VICTORY DRIVE IN, WEST HOLLYWOOD, CALIFORNIA

Michael arrived at the Griffith Observatory at 7:00 p.m. Although never having visited the star gazing site, there were parts of the observatory that he knew quite well.

Carefully, he walked in the footsteps of his hero. James Dean's classic movie progressed through his mind frame by frame. He replayed the knife fight scene, perched on Griffith's lower level, step by step, an imaginary switch blade in his hand. He peered through the giant Art Deco doors at the main entrance, reciting Jim Stark's lines perfectly, imagining the police with guns drawn and aimed in his direction.

Standing on the roof in front of the observatory's telescope, Michael marveled at the sheer size of Los Angeles. Lines of street lights stretched for 30 miles to the west extinguished by the Pacific Ocean, north to the San Fernando Valley, and east to Pasadena. Powered by millions of kilowatts, the City of Angels seemed perfectly angelic.

Leaving for the Victory Drive-In, with his confidence restored, Michael sped downhill toward West Hollywood, arriving at the theater just as the previews started.

Guiding the Cadillac carefully past the endless rows of iron posts, topped with clunky metal speaker boxes, he made his way to the back of the drive-in and parked . . . the only car on the back row.

The solitude assured him there would be no distractions. He would study the performances, analyze the story flow, and catalog the scenes in his mind. In front of him, the giant Victory Screen, with its colossal Western mural on the street side, beckoned to all the prom-ise of movie magic and an escape from reality for a few hours. Lined row by row inside the theater, the occupants of over 600 cars read-ied for the suspense of Hitchcock's thriller.

With a bag of popcorn and a Barg's Root Beer, he sat on the hood of the Cadillac while the opening scenes of the movie began to flash on the screen.

9:45 P.M., THE GRIFFITH OBSERVATORY, LOS ANGELES, CALIFORNIA

So let me see if I understand you correctly Doctor," Annie answered the director of the observatory. "During a supernova event, the remnants of the gravitational collapse of a large star are called neutron stars?"

"Very good, Annie!" The director praised her.

The exasperated crew stood frozen beside the giant Zeiss refractor telescope, panting from having run through the entire observatory again. Annie held up her index finger, asking them for quiet as she responded to the director.

"Within the Relativistic Kinematics framework as it defines mass, any gravitational collapse of a star over five solar masses will create a black hole?"

"Excellent!" The director smiled, clapping her hands exuberantly, elated to have received some intelligent questions about the observatory's work on discovering how black holes are formed in space.

It could be worse. Billy thought with gallows humor. *Glad she didn't find any loose screwdrivers lying around. That telescope could be in pieces by now.*

"You must be Billy," the director asked with a smile.

Billy just shook his head in acknowledgment, still out of breath from climbing the stairs.

"Your sister is quite intelligent."

"Isn't this refractor the best thing you've ever seen Billy?" Annie posed the question, obviously excited.

"Oh, yeah, it's great Annie," he tried hard not to sound sarcastic, "but don't you think it would be a good idea to let the director go now?" He looked at the director, raising his eyebrows. "They're closing in a few minutes and I'm sure she has other work to take care of."

"Well, yes, I suppose you're right young man," the Director agreed, patting Annie on the head, "but it's been such a pleasure talking about the heavens with Annie."

As they ran down the steps, leaping into the Fairlane, Billy groaned inwardly. *I think our chances of getting to the drive in before that movie's over . . . just went down a black hole."*

DANNY WHITE

9:50 P.M., THE VICTORY DRIVE-IN,
WEST HOLLYWOOD, CALIFORNIA

On the hood of the Cadillac, Michael felt at home. The theater reminded him of the Drive-In back in Iowa Falls, where he attended so many movies as a small boy. It brought back memories of better times. Iowa, and the life he left behind seemed so far away now, but it was closer than what he wanted to admit. The pangs of guilt kept creeping in and his conflicted emotions meandered their way into his consciousness, stealing his attention away from the movie.

He pushed the situation out of his thoughts, but it wouldn't stay there. What he did was wrong, dead wrong and completely selfish. He wanted to call and at least try to explain things but he couldn't get himself to do it. He wished he would have talked to his dad before he left, but it was far too late for that now.

Michael stared back into the giant screen but couldn't concentrate. So lost in thought and caught up in struggling with his feelings over the last twenty minutes, he hadn't noticed the red Mercury Dragger parked on his left or the Chevy that had smoothly parked at his right. A tap on the shoulder caused his reflections to flee.

"What's happenin' Big Wheel?" A voice with a foreign accent croaked behind the burning end of a Camel no filter. "Hell of a car for a guy in a leather jacket and a t-shirt." The tall man with a pocked face walked from Michael's left, crossing in front of him, eyeballing the car.

"You must be the only doctor or lawyer, or whatever you are, in the whole city of Los Angeles in a grungy leather jacket with a car like this."

Michael shifted nervously. "Hey I'm not looking for troub–"

The man cut Michael off in mid-sentence.

"No. I've got it," he said underneath a devilish grin. "You catch me more as an Indian kind of a guy, or maybe a Triumph. Yeah, that's it an' you're just borrowin' this car for a while."

Feigning the role of suddenly being enlightened, the pale faced tough looked for agreement among the others in the dark, who were staying just out of the light.

The lurid man looked through the square he made of his hands, playing the role of a casting director. "I can see it now. You're more of the Marlon Brando type. Maybe you just found some sucker and traded your old Triumph for this beauty."

The performance drew muted chortles from the gang still lurking in the shadows.

Hitchcock's movie sunk into the background. Michael was surrounded by the hoodlums and they weren't there for the movie.

10:35 P.M., THE VICTORY DRIVE IN, WEST HOLLYWOOD, CALIFORNIA

DJ pulled into the center lane of the drive-in that divided the northern and southern sections, coming to a stop just to the right of the concession stand. The final scenes of the movie raced across the screen, in heart stopping Hitchcock fashion.

"We'll have to split up," Jill said, pulling her hair into a ponytail. "There's going to be a stampede of cars trying to get out of here any minute."

Billy agreed, pointing in the direction of the screen with authority.

"DJ," Billy ordered. "Take Annie with you and work to the front. Jill and I will make our way to the back of the lot and we'll meet back here."

DJ and Annie took off through the complex toward the big screen, zigzagging their way through the cars.

Billy and Jill worked row by row behind them, running horizontally through the theater trying to avoid getting between the screen and the movie goers but there was little time to be polite. Billy knew it could be their one and only chance to find the Cadillac and the tapes.

They continued sifting through the Fords, Chevys, Desotos, and Packard's. They checked the convertibles, and hot rods, tiptoeing past the foggy covered windows of draggers, woodies, and trucks parked side by side in the passion pit.

There were families, lovers, sleepers, and wide-eyed movie zombies caught in frozen stares. The imprint of cinema action blazed on their corneas, locked in the drama unfolding on the massive screen. It seemed every vehicle type known to the free world was at the Victory but no Cadillac Brougham, and no Michael Minton.

As the credits rolled, so did the cars, leaving behind an enormous cloud of dust. The mass exodus of patrons reminded Billy of the closing scenes from, *The Ten Commandments*. Disoriented in the swirling updrafts of automobile exhaust and dust, running became a walk. Suddenly, more important than finding the Cadillac amidst the bewildering morass was the quest to find each other. Failure and dejection gripped Billy as he labored through the traffic jam. Only a few straggling cars remained in the back section of the theater. He began to question himself.

He should have been here! Michael wouldn't have left before the end of the movie... maybe he didn't come at all?

"Billy," Jill's soft, yet disturbed voice sailed over his right shoulder. "Is that somebody lying against the fence or a bag of trash?"

Twenty-five yards away, Billy saw an amorphous outline of something, or someone lying against the perimeter fence. It soon became apparent that it was no bag of trash as he approached the motionless body. He knelt down, then, reached out to turn over the slumped figure, beaten unconscious. The victim's bloody and swollen face took his breath away.

Five blocks away, the Cadillac's right turn signal flashed. Rounding the corner, the man with the pock-marked face hissed . . . *Spokojnoj.* Then, he flicked his spent Camel to the curb of Victory Boulevard and slowly melted into the dark night.

11:00 P.M., THE VICTORY DRIVE IN, HOLLYWOOD, CALIFORNIA

He's alive!"

Billy was shaking, finally getting a pulse with his index finger, pressing tightly on Michael's jugular vein.

Jill grabbed Annie's trembling hand, "come with me quick Annie, we need a wet towel and some ice." They returned out of breath, carrying a towel and two large popcorn cups full of ice

DJ took a pillow from the Fairlane and put it under Michael's head, gently laying the cold towel on his face. His nose poured blood, his forehead slashed, and his cheeks were raw with scrapes. An enormous bruise bloomed beneath an eye as he slowly began to come to.

Looking up through the blur Michael thought he saw two figures, familiar somehow.

"Michael!" Billy said, gently shaking his limp arms.

The voice. Michael thought hazily. *I know that voice from somewhere.*

"Michael. It's Billy Daniels and Darrel Evans. We're here to help you."

As their faces began to materialize, Michael started to think the fight must have been a bad dream. Now, people he once knew from high school were starting to show up for good measure.

"Billy . . . ? Michael wobbled, "w'wha . . . whath . . . ur . . . you . . . doin . . . hrr? Whur, where's tha . . . the Cad . . . Cadillac?"

"Not now, Michael." Billy answered holding his hand underneath Michael's head, glancing at DJ in utter disbelief. "Let's get you out of here."

With a fresh pack of ice on his eye, they helped Michael into the car and left for the safety of Jill's house in Bel Air.

Michael remained silent. A freight train with its engineer leaning on the air horn was running through his brain. He hung his head out the window as they rolled down the Colorado Freeway, staring at the highway as it sped underneath the car in a washy blur.

14

FEBRUARY 7, 12:30 A.M., THE LOVELLE RESIDENCE. 820 LINDA FLORA WAY, BEL AIR, CALIFORNIA

Arriving at the Lovelle residence, the exhausted, rag tag bunch unloaded their luggage, drained from the day's events.

After showing Annie to her room, Jill packed two more bags of ice for Michael's face, which was looking more and more like twenty miles of bad road as each minute passed by. With the ice bags, a bottle of aspirin, and a glass of water sitting on his nightstand, she shut the door on Michael's room and walked into the hallway.

"Join me on the veranda to talk about a plan for tomorrow?" She glanced at Billy with her beautiful blue eyes.

Billy, still jittery after finding Michael nodded; his mind full of questions.

DJ glanced wryly at his buddy as they passed each other going opposite directions in the hallway. "Don't do anything I wouldn't do."

Billy rolled his eyes ignoring DJ's snicker as he walked through the french doors that opened onto the spacious patio.

Billy gazed over the moonlit Pacific in the far distance, it couldn't have been a nicer evening. The fact that the Cadillac was gone, again, didn't seem to bother him as the breeze swept through the hills from the shore below. Finding Michael seemed to reduce the dilemma of the Caddy's whereabouts for the moment to a minor rumble in his thoughts.

"Would you like a glass of lemonade?" Jill offered, walking back from the kitchen with two glasses in hand.

"Thank you kindly." Billy's thoughts swiftly returned to the here-and-now as he reached for one of the tumblers.

"Wow, real lemons?"

"Yes, directly from the lemon factory in our back yard," Jill said sarcastically with a laugh, looking past the pool into the wooded area beyond it. "We have a couple of trees that keep us in lemonade the whole year. My grandparents gave the trees to my mother and father when they built this home."

"Sounds like a very 'country' thing to do," Billy reckoned, taking another drink. "In Iowa it would likely be a pair of apple trees!"

"Apple trees are wonderful too. My family is from the country after all." She explained, "I think the lemon trees are one of my grandfather's little 'country' reminders. He always used to say; "we've come from the land, never forget that. We're Kansas folk after all!"

"Your family is from Kansas?" Billy asked, surprised there could be any connection between the mansion he was sitting in, and the state of Kansas. Billy nervously stretched out his legs on the patio sofa, nearly knocking over his drink. He grabbed for it, and in desperation said, "How do people from Kansas come to live in a place like this? I've never seen a house this big."

"Oh, it's a long story Billy," she looked away to the moon's reflection on the pool, "would bore you to tears."

"I'm not that tired! Besides, I may never get the chance to relax by a pool with a beautiful girl like you again in my life!" Billy abruptly stopped, unsure of if he had gone too far, holding his breath.

"So you're twisting my arm to tell you the story?"

"Yes! I'm twisting your arm already!" Inspired by his apparent success, Billy reached for her arm and mimicked twisting it.

"OK then." Jill laughed. "It all started in downtown Manhattan . . . Kansas that is, way back in the 1800s when my Great Grandparents opened Lovelle Mercantile. It was pretty much a general store, if you want to call it that. My family owned the store until the stock market crash of 1929. We lost everything."

"My Grandparents on my mom's side lost their home in 1929 too." Billy interjected. "That's another thing we have in common I suppose."

She answered, a tinge of shyness in her voice. "I think before the story is over, we might have quite a lot more in common."

Billy didn't care, as long she stayed sitting there looking lovely in the moonlight, she could be reading the phone book as far as he was concerned.

"And so my Grandparents and my Mom and Dad, who were newly

married, decided to leave "the Little Apple," as my dad likes to call it. When they got to California in 1930, they moved into my Aunt Patricia's garage. The little garage was their home while my Father and Grandfather looked for work. One day my Aunt told my Grandfather that she heard about a staging company working for Warner Brothers that was looking for help on a film set. At the end of the day's work, my Grandfather noticed that the company he was working for didn't do a very good job. So, he came home and told everyone that there was going to be a new family company started!"

"A new company?" Billy wondered. "What were they going to start it with?"

"Good question!" Jill laughed.

"He told my Dad to sell his car and that the whole family would share the old Lovelle mercantile box truck. So, Dad sold the car and they started the company with ninety-five dollars."

"Ninety-five dollars! I've put that much into batteries for my old broken down car this year!" Billy laughed contagiously, drawing Jill in with him.

"That's how they started 'Lovelle Film Services,' our family business." Jill stated, concluding with a flourish of her lemonade glass.

"We're very proud to say that last year we worked on every motion picture, in one way or the other, that was nominated for an Academy Award."

Billy shook his head in amazement.

"And by the way, that's how I know Rose," she explained. "Rose has worked for our business since before I was born . . . she's kind of like a second mom."

"I knew it had to be something like that. You must be very close." Billy thanked her for sharing the story. "It reminds me of what my dad used to say; 'Son, it's the mid-western way. People from our part of the world are survivors, plain and simple.'"

"You seem like a survivor to me Billy." Jill smiled into her glass.

Billy felt the blood surging through him, filling him with a sizzling energy, so much that he felt he could've jogged to the beach and back. He was captivated by the beautiful young woman's eyes, and the way her eyelashes swooped over her cheek when she blinked. The rosy color of her lips against her tan completed the picture of perfection that he saw in her. What a dream! She couldn't have been nicer and did everything she could to help them over the last two nights. Without her, they would have been completely lost.

Her combination of elegant beauty and hard-nosed determination attracted him like no one before. She handled herself with grace, yet was not afraid to take off on a dead run through a dusty drive-in, looking for someone she didn't even know, just to try and help.

Since the moment he met her, she filled his every thought that wasn't devoted to finding the car. He was trying hard to hide it, but he was terrible at that sort of thing. He twisted his head away from Jill's soft gaze and instead, gazed out to the ocean.

"What are you looking at Billy? You've drifted away on me."

"You know, I had never seen the ocean until yesterday," he admitted, a little embarrassed. "But it was almost like I didn't see it at the pier.

I was so distracted by everything that was going on with trying to find Michael that I completely missed it. I feel like I'm looking at it now for the very first time. It is truly amazing."

Listening to Billy speak about the ocean gave her butterflies. His sincere, heartfelt words moved her.

"Really?" She said nicely, hiding her unexpected rush of emotion. "The ocean is beautiful isn't it?"

There was an easy silence as a calm breeze weaved its way through the palm trees and around the pool. A radio played through the veranda sound system, but Billy hadn't noticed it during their conversation. The silence brought it to life.

"This is da' Spaceman coming at ya from the super galactic radio rocket ship X.R.K.T., the station that plays whatever it wants and before ya can hear it anywhere else." The wild disc jockey's voice seemed to fly out of the speakers even though the radio was barely turned up.

"Tonight da' Spaceman gotta new one fo' ya. For the first time on the radio anywhere, I said annyy-where, right here tonight fo' all you boys and girls. Here it come! All you Zombies out there in Spaceland, lookout! It's Santo and Johnny . . . "Sleepwalk!"

"My track record on finding the Cadillac hasn't been so great, huh?" Billy changed the subject, sensing that maybe they should talk about what they were going to do in the morning. He chuckled, "I'll tell you one thing I'm good at . . . losing it!"

"We're going to find it Billy, don't worry," she assured him, "you're doing a good job in a tough situation."

"What's your take on this predicament Jill?"

"I think we should talk to Michael in the morning and see what he knows. Maybe he can tell us what happened and get a direction from there."

She picked up the glasses, sitting them softly on the serving tray. "Don't fret Billy, it will all work out. Let's get some sleep, OK? We're going to need it tomorrow."

They both stood to return inside, awkwardly face to face with only the tray between them. Billy thought about what it would be like to kiss her all day, but didn't want to take a chance on ruining every-thing, just when she was starting to warm up to him.

Before he could lose his nerve, he leaned over, kissed her lightly on the cheek, and whispered. "Thank you for your help today. You've been wonderful."

Jill's eyes brightened, reaching up to feel his warmth on her cheek.

"You're welcome." She replied softly. "We'll get a plan together in the morning, alright?"

"Yes. Yes we will." Billy nodded assuredly. "Goodnight."

★★★★★★★★★★★★★★★★★★★★★★★★★★★★★★

FEBRUARY 7, 1959
A HOT ROD AND A RUSSIAN ROCKET

★★★★★★★★★★★★★★★★★★★★★★★★★★★★

15

7:00 A.M., THE LOVELLE RESIDENCE, BEL AIR, CALIFORNIA

Billy rolled out of the unfamiliar king-sized feather down bed early. Tossing and turning most of the night, he alternated between musing on Jill and wondering how they were going to find the Cadillac. All of it added up to a severe lack of sleep.

He walked around the giant bedroom that was nearly the size of the living room at his parent's house and peered out the window. Pulling the curtain back gently, he saw Jill waving goodbye to an older couple in a new Mercedes-Benz convertible.

Must be the folks. He reckoned, watching the stately cabriolet pass through the iron gates of the Lovelle driveway.

Returning to his bed to make the covers and straighten his room, a beautiful wooden clock, mounted to the wall and built in the shape of the sun, read 7:00 a.m.

It's 9:00 a.m. in Clear Lake. He thought. *"I'm sure Mr. Minton will be in."*

Within moments, Minton was on the phone.

"Mr. Minton, Billy here. How are you?"

Fred juggled the telephone and a grease gun while trying to locate a shop towel.

"Hello. Billy? Are you O.K.?"

"We're doing just fine . . . made it to California safe and sound."

Fred asked apprehensively. "Is there any news about Michael?"

"We found him." Billy reported. "He's been in some sort of a fight, but he's OK.

"Thank God he's alright." Fred's voice cracked, his emotions coming to the surface.

"The bad news is . . ." Billy paused, "that we think the Cadillac's been stolen again."

"What?" Fred asked bewildered. "How in the world did that happen?"

"We're not sure, to tell you the truth," Billy said uneasily. "All we know right now is that somebody beat him up pretty bad and the car is missing."

Billy took a few minutes to explain to Fred what happened. "Would you like to speak to Michael?"

Fred replied gratefully. "I would like nothing more."

Billy knocked on Michael's door, waking him up so the father and son could talk in private. The circumstances were tense. Billy wondered if Fred would say anything to him in regard to whom he stole the car from. If Fred declined, it was going to be his job to do it. Fifteen minutes later, he knew the answer to the question.

Michael walked out of the room, ashen faced, staring at the tile floor. He handed the phone to Billy. "My dad wants to talk to you."

"Yes, Mr. Minton?"

"Billy," he said earnestly, "I appreciate everything you've done and I'm grateful. Michael wants to make it up you, but he doesn't know how."

"Let's just hope we can find that car, Mr. Minton." Billy said with a nervous chuckle. "Right now were both in the soup."

Fred gathered himself after being choked up by the conversation. "There was something I forgot to tell you a few minutes ago Billy."

"If it's about money," Billy guessed, "we're doing fine. In fact we'll bring a lot of it back to you."

"No, no it's not that at all." Fred assured him, brushing away any concern about the money. "There was a man named Stoneman who stopped by here Thursday while I was out. His card says he's from the Office of Broadcast Security in Washington. I'm sorry to say but Eddie spilled the beans about this whole situation. The agent said he wanted to speak to you and aimed to take those tapes."

"Really? Why would the agent want the tapes?"

"Not sure . . . said it was part of the investigation into the plane crash."

Billy thought a moment. "I find it hard to believe that the music I recorded would have anything to do with the crash."

Fred agreed. "The whole thing sounds unusual that's for sure. Eddie said the guy looked like trouble and took the contact information that you gave me. I didn't appreciate it very much, I can tell you that."

Fred stopped, cautiously as if remembering something else.

"Mr. Minton?" Billy asked into the silent receiver.

"Yes Billy, there's one last thing. I hate to add anything else to your plate, but according to Eddie, it sounded like that Agent was coming to Los Angeles after you."

Billy wondered, making his way to the kitchen after hanging up with Minton.

Why would the government send an agent all the way to Los Angeles to take the tapes from me?

The sound of Jill singing Doris Day's, *Que Sera Sera* rang down the hallway as she made breakfast. Jill was the only bright spot in a disturbing string of thoughts he was wrestling with.

If they were so interested in the tapes for the crash investigation, why not try and call me first? Or leave a phone number with Fred?

DANNY WHITE

10:00 A.M., THE LOVELLE'S,
BEL AIR, CALIFORNIA

The winter sun hung low in the Southern California sky, burning the last hint of mist from the hills that surrounded Bel Air. It was a late morning but they needed the sleep, and Michael needed recovery time.

From the very beginning, their journey to California was like living in the vortex of a tornado and running as fast as they could go to. After the disturbing events at the Victory Drive-In the prior evening, the whole crew was bushed.

Michael was silent as he approached the kitchen table that Jill set with scrambled eggs, bacon, and fresh fruit. He sat gingerly on the closest chair he could grab on to as the sun revealed an eye still puffy and swollen. Michael looked miserable with the scratches on this arms and face appearing much worse than the night before.

It was an awkward and uncomfortable moment for everyone, but mostly for Michael. He had a black eye, a busted lower lip, and what felt like three broken ribs. Beyond the obvious physical beating, what hurt most was his wounded pride. The humiliation and embarrassment that he faced, sitting at the table eating breakfast with the nephew of the person he stole the car from, was almost too much to bear. Finally, he gave up trying to drink his glass of orange juice, and in a barely audible murmur said; "I'm sorry."

His voice was fragile from the drubbing and filled with heartfelt remorse.

"I've caused all of you a lot of problems with what I've done and I truly regret bringing you all into this. I can't explain my actions in taking the car. I just lost it for a while. I'm not making excuses, it's just the truth."

An uneasy silence hung around the table like an oppressive shroud. Michael continued.

"I'll turn myself in if you'll be kind enough to drive me to the police station, maybe they can help us find the Cadillac."

The quiet stretched on for a few more long seconds, broken only by the occasional clank of a fork or knife grazing the Lovelle's bone china dinnerware.

"No, you don't need to do that." Billy said kindly with conviction. "You're a good guy, I know that Michael. I've made my share of mistakes in this mess too."

Billy looked at DJ and Annie. "We didn't come all the way to California to see you go to jail. We could have called the police to come after you in Iowa." He focused on buttering his toast, not looking at Jill as he admitted his bad judgment. "I'm in the hot seat too. If I hadn't taken the car to the show on Monday, none of this would have happened. There's plenty of blame to go around but none of that's gonna help us now."

Jill nodded somberly, understanding Billy's anxiety level over the past few days. At the table, Billy took a moment to explain to Michael that there was another reason why they came to California.

Michael was stunned with the news, putting his elbows on the table and throbbing head into his hands above the plate of food he had yet to touch.

"You've got to be kidding me? My dad didn't say anything about it."

"Believe me Michael, I wish I was kidding."

"I am so sorry. Jeez." Michael stared around at the circle of friends, pained memory reflected in his eyes. "I wanted to go to that show too, but with the alert, I was up to my neck working the tow truck."

"Michael." Billy straightened. "Tell us what happened at the drive-in last night."

The group suddenly quieted once again. Annie stopped scraping her toast, burnt to a crisp as a result of her "help" in the kitchen.

Billy leaned forward, emphasizing the significance of his admonishment. "Tell us anything and everything. Any detail you might have, no matter how small might help."

Michael slowly picked up his glass of orange juice, sipping it carefully through his split lip and thought for a moment.

He began slowly. "Yesterday after I left Griffith Park, I drove the Cadillac to the theater." A confused look replaced his air of concentration, surrounded by expectant faces. "How did you know I was there?"

Jill responded swiftly, anxious to get to the rest of the details. "My friend Rose called us after she talked to you yesterday."

"You mean Rose from the El Rancho Hotel in New Mexico?"

"Yes." Jill confirmed.

"Well then how in the world did you guys know I was going to The El Rancho?" Michael muttered, now completely intrigued.

"We didn't." Annie replied, importantly. "We figured it out along the way."

Michael groaned, running his scratched-up hands alongside his head, feeling the goose-egg sized bump that only seemed to be getting bigger. "Wow, I even feel worse now. I tried to get out of town without leaving a clue and I couldn't even do that right."

"Michael," Billy tried to get him to refocus. "We really need to know what happened at the Drive-In."

Michael winced, trying to clear the cobwebs spun in his head, trapping his thoughts.

"I parked at the back of the theater minding my own business, watching the movie. The next thing I know a bunch of thugs and their cars surrounded me. He felt for the bump on his head again. "This guy named Kenny, no, wait a minute, it was a weird name. Ken, Krantz, Keiler, Kre . . . Kreiger. That's it . . . speaks with an accent, he's the guy who took the car."

Billy nodded, encouraging him forward.

"I got sucker-punched from behind. I didn't have a chance," he said, moving his hand from the knot on his head to the bruise on his sternum.

The events began straggling back, making their way through the cotton balls behind his eyes.

"After I hit the ground, this guy Kreiger put his knee on my chest and said something about how a thief knows a thief . . . said he knew the Cadillac wasn't my car."

Billy pressed. "Are you sure that this guy's name is Krieger?"

"That's what one of the guys called him, when I was on the ground, just before he knocked me out. The next thing I remember was seeing you and DJ."

Billy continued to push for any new morsel of information. "Is there anything else?"

"Yeah," Michael shook his head. "The money in my wallet is gone, and all of my clothes were in the car too."

DJ finished with his breakfast. He sat with his arms folded, a look of skepticism clear on his face. Throughout the entire conversation, he listened to Michael, keeping a tight lip, but wasn't nearly as forgiving as Billy. If he concluded that Michael was withholding anything, he was going to take great pleasure in making his good eye match his bad one. It was DJ's turn for a cross examination.

"You said you were surrounded by cars?"

"Yeah, there were cars on both sides."

"Can you describe anything about the cars . . . anything at all?"

Michael closed his eyes as he grappled to free the information from his pounding temple.

"I remember one of them being souped up and the other one cus-tomized. The screamer was a newer car, kind of looked stock but in a tough way, like it was built that way from the factory."

DJ prodded him for more details. "Go on."

"It was black or maybe dark green. The back top half of the rear panel was painted white, and the wheels were painted white too . . . I think"

DJ gave it a second. "So the newer car was modified but looked stock, sorta bulky maybe?"

Michael wracked his scattered brain, trying to recall the images.

"Yeah, kinda looked like Barry Jacobi's car back home. It had some sort of emblem on the back of the car by the taillight . . . a pair of flags with something written underneath it."

DJ recalled Jacobi's car from Clear Lake. "A Chevy?"

Michael replied. "Maybe . . . I think so."

DJ got up from the table and stared at the floor as he paced the Lovelle kitchen. Then, he stopped and looked up, realizing they were on to something. He knew Michael's was telling the truth.

"Michael. The emblem was on the back top half of the car, in the sec-tion painted white. Is that correct?"

"Yeah, kinda forward of the tail light."

"Could the writing below the flags on the emblem have been *Fuel Injection* by any chance?"

Michael frowned again. Grasping for memories from the night before. "That coulda been it, yeah . . . Fuel Injection! That's it."

"Wow." DJ ran the fingers on both of his hands through his hair. "Sounds like it was a '57 Chevy, but not your car lot variety."

DJ's pace quickened. Every head in the room tracked him as he traversed the kitchen floor, back and forth. Then he stopped.

"The only car I can think of with that kind of a paint job, that's Fuel Injected would be a Black Widow. It's an extremely rare machine." DJ quickly searched his memory for similar cars.

"A Corvette comes with a fuel injected option, but from what you've just described, the car was definitely not a `Vette."

Billy was following DJ's assessment precisely. "Black Widows are supposed to be a NASCAR only machine, right?"

DJ's pacing began again.

"Yeah, exactly. It's a super fast car. Wouldn't know how anyone would get one for the street, but this is California after all."

"Simple," Billy surmised. "He stole it. He could be a runner too."

"What's a runner?" Jill asked, looking from Billy to DJ and back.

"A drag racer." Billy responded, sure that his friend's deduction was on the mark.

DJ added, shaking his head thoughtfully. "Anyone with a car like that on the street is going to be looking to put notches in his belt with it."

"Great," Billy clapped his hands a single time, nodding at DJ in silent thanks. "We're looking for a guy named Kreiger, or similar name. He speaks with a foreign accent and drives a black and white '57 Chevy Black Widow. Right?"

"That's my best bet pal." DJ confirmed.

"Is there anything else Michael?" Billy asked.

"It's all coming back in pieces. I'll keep you up date as the clouds start to go away."

Billy encouraged everyone to get a move on. "Let's hit the road then and see what we can dig up. We've got some serious looking to do."

There was a burst of energy in the new formed gang of five. Rested and well fed, they jumped into the Fairlane and headed toward Sunset Boulevard, ready to begin the search anew.

16

11:00 A.M., SUNSET BOULEVARD, HOLLYWOOD, CALIFORNIA

DJ drove down the Sunset Strip as Bill Haley and The Comet's "*13 Women*" blasted from the radio. Ogling the girls walking along the storied boulevard, he wished he could find a couple of hours to go "chase the skirts." His mind drifted back to the work at hand, set on finding the black and white Chevy.

Where would a guy with a Black Widow be hanging around town? He asked himself.

Palm trees lining the streets like giant Roman columns, waved in the morning breeze and slowly disappeared in the Fairlane's rear window. DJ glanced over his shoulder, throwing his voice into the back seat.

"Hey Jill. Where do people go to race in this town?"

She thought for a moment, sitting alongside Annie, who was studying the street map quietly. Michael, eyes closed, leaned into a corner.

"There are the racetracks of course. But you're talking about street racing, right?"

"Yup, drag racing to be exact."

Jill shrugged. "The evening news always has reports about how dangerous the illegal street races are over on Colorado Boulevard in Glendale."

"Colorado Boulevard, huh?" DJ rapped his fingers on the steering wheel, "that sounds like a good place to start to me. What say you, Billy?"

"Well, since I know as much about this city as you do, I think it's a grand idea." He turned to the back seat. "Jill, where's Colorad–

Annie interrupted her brother, determined to be useful, the street map that she wrangled from the desk clerk at The Roosevelt at the end of her fingertips.

"Drive past the light coming up, that's Gower. You'll be looking for Western Avenue North. Make a right on Los Feliz and follow that up to San Fernando Road. Look for West Colorado just past Vine."

Annie looked toward Jill with a smile.

"Way to go, Annie!" Jill exuded in a congratulatory tone, teasing her with a laugh. "Are you sure you're not a tour guide here by any chance?"

Billy's thankful smile met her in the rear view mirror.

DJ looked back at Annie, flushed with the praise. "I'll need that one more time, sweetheart."

DANNY WHITE

12:00 P.M., GLENDALE, CALIFORNIA

They cruised Colorado Boulevard, looking for any sign of the Cadillac or the Black Widow. They hit up gas station attendants, restaurant waiters and waitresses, burger joint operators, and auto repair shop grease monkeys. Nobody knew anything about a guy named Krieger or a black and white Chevy.

After searching for over an hour and a half, DJ saw a sign painted in bright green and white at the opposite corner of the street that caught his attention.

Bettery's Tire and Wheel: We'll get you there fast."

"Hang on everybody! U turn coming up!" DJ sang out, pulling the wheel hard to the left.

Billy grabbed the dash pad, and everyone in the back seat latched onto whatever they could find before being flung against the doors. The Fairlane spun easily, smoothly coasting into the parking lot of the little garage.

DJ walked into the store, and up to the counter. A smallish, grubby shop clerk peered around his broad shoulders.

"Is that your Fairlane out there?"

DJ grinned. "That's right."

"Boss ride . . . sounds like a stuffer. Whatcha' got in it man?"

"It's just a six banger." DJ's smile got a little bigger.

"Yeah right and tomorrow's Christmas. You runners are all the same . . . cloak and dagger twenty-four seven. What can I do for ya Daddy-O?"

"I'm looking for a guy named Kreiger, drives a '57 Chevy Black Widow. Seen him around?"

A flicker of alarm crossed the clerk's face when he heard the name. DJ knew he was on to something as the friendly disposition of the auto parts clerk suddenly became strained.

"I've never heard of him man."

"Really?" DJ casually leaned on the counter, reaching into a back pocket of his dungarees. "Would twenty Washington's help your memory?"

The clerk squeaked, moving over to hover by the register. "Look man, I don't want any trouble. "Who wants to know, anyhow?"

"Just me." DJ's tone was cool, ignoring the friction, shoving the twenty toward the register. "There won't be any trouble. I was never here."

"You know," the clerk cleared his throat noisily, "he comes in here for parts sometimes, but uh, he's not someone I hang out with. You should just forget that you ever heard his name and leave him alone."

"That all may be true," DJ said mildly, slapping another twenty on the counter, sensing a cache' of information could be had. "But I've still got business with the man."

He eyed the crisp, forty bucks lying on the counter. It was too much to pass up.

"His name is Kreiger Koslov . . . they call him *The Cosmonaut*. He's goes for pinks. If titles aren't on the line, he won't run."

"I need more than that for forty dollars." DJ straightened up, giving the mousy clerk a full appreciation of his considerable size.

The clerk wiped his sweaty forehead with a soiled handkerchief, pulled from a front pocket. His eyes darted quickly around the empty storefront.

"Koslov and his gang make the circuit through the city looking for action. Any car he wins gets cut up and disappears." He risked another look at the money under DJ's stony fist. "Some people say he steals cars too but no one talks about it. He'll be around town tonight for sure."

"And where around town would that be?" DJ asked quietly.

"I don't know exactly where man! I'm not in his gang."

It was clear to the clerk that DJ wasn't going to leave.

"Try Glen Oaks in the Valley or Foothill Boulevard in Pasadena maybe. Sometimes he'll hang out at the Village Inn here in Glendale then cruise over to Downey. That's it. That's all I know." The man's voice had turned into a squeak.

DJ slowly took his hand off of the money.

The flabbergasted clerk darted for the cash and pointed to the front door. He then turned and bolted for the back of the store.

"Goodbye sir. Thank you for shopping at Bettery's. Have a nice day."

DJ raised his voice and the clerk stopped. "Why do they call this guy The Cosmonaut?"

The clerk scowled over his shoulder. "Because his car is faster than a Russian rocket, that's why."

The door swung wildly behind him and the clerk disappeared among the racks of racing slicks and white walls.

DJ returned the good wishes, "and a nice day to you . . . man."

He figured as much. The fairly juvenile adventure they started in Iowa, suddenly took a dark and dangerous turn.

No longer chasing a harmless guy from Clear Lake, now they had to find a real car thief and swindler. To make matters worse, the guy was a sneaky Red with a gang.

The Cosmonaut. DJ whistled appreciatively as he made his way back to the car. *City of Angels my rear end.*

1:30 P.M., BOB'S BIG BOY, PASADENA, CALIFORNIA

Sitting in a corner booth at Bob's Big Boy, a slim, cheerful waitress brought everyone burgers, dripping with just-melted cheese, oozing hamburger relish, and mayonnaise under thick slabs of tomato. She slipped the plates expertly around the table and asked. "Anything else, kids?" The group murmured their thanks and dug in.

The brightly lit, multi-colored jukebox remote at the end of the table, finally got the best of Annie's curiosity. She reached for the Seeburg Select-O-Matic Wallbox, popped in a nickel, and pressed A-11. The Coasters: *Yakety Yak*.

During their lunch, DJ told everyone about the enlightening conversation with the clerk at the tire store. The sobering reality of the change in the game brought about a similar change of mood at the table. He shoved his plate away, crossed his arms, and assessed the situation.

"First of all, this is not a situation for women and children to be tangled up in." He glanced at Jill and Annie before directing his comments to Billy. "I say we take Annie and Jill back to Bel Air. Then, the three of us should come back into town tonight and turn over the rock this guy's hidin' under."

Annie said nothing, her mouth still full of vanilla shake.

"Really?" Jill responded, the tone of her voice a warning. "Is that a fact? It's so very nice that you took the time to make my mind up for me DJ."

Dang it! Billy tensed, willing DJ with his eyes to change course and shut up.

"For your information," Jill continued. "I have no intention of going home to stay put . . . and by the way," she flashed a glance toward Annie, "we've made a pretty good team getting you guys around town all day. Isn't that right Annie?"

Annie didn't answer. Instead, she turned around, locked eyes with her big brother and said: "We're going."

"Gosh darn it, DJ!!"

Billy slammed his fist on the table with finality. Spoons and forks rattled to the black and white checkered tile that covered Bob's floor like a polished chess board.

Billy knew better than to argue with the girls. He wasn't going to try and convince Annie otherwise, and didn't want to get on the wrong side of Jill.

"We're all staying together to see where this leads then right?" He said raising an eyebrow, noting with pleasure that Jill had turned to him with a grateful smile.

"Are you in, Michael?"

"I got us into this," Michael mumbled, a French fry teetering on his numb lip. "If I can help get us out I will."

"OK, good. Now *I'm* going to say something." Billy drew himself up, his straight eyebrows winging in a stern line across his forehead. "If everybody's going, then we stay together. No exceptions . . . period."

He turned to Jill and Annie pointedly. "I can't make either of you stay home, but what I can do is turn the car around and drive back to Iowa right now. We run as a team or it's over . . . no wandering off." He glanced at Annie again. "Got it?"

Everyone at the table nodded, and a few seconds of quiet followed.

Jill offered, trying to turn the tense energy hanging in the dead air into something useful. "Calling Rose might be of some help. She's got a good track record so far."

In the payphone booth outside of Bob's, Jill wasted little time in getting Rose on the horn.

"We need to know if you've heard of a guy named Kreiger Koslov." Jill asked, half-knowing that Rose wouldn't have connections with that kind of crowd. The reply came back as expected.

Jill continued, giving Rose the details that DJ learned about Koslov.

"Sounds like a dangerous guy," Rose cautioned. "Maybe it's time to call it quits on trying to find the car?"

"At this point it's more about the tapes Rose. We need to find those tapes . . . they're important."

Rose tried to persuade her. "I know they are love. Cars can be replaced of course, and it would be a shame about the recordings, but not the end of the world."

"We're being careful, and you know me Rose, I wouldn't do anything to get myself into trouble."

Rose was familiar with Jill's tone of voice and knew Jill Lovelle like her own daughter. She was beautiful and intelligent, but her head was as hard as a coffin nail. Once she got into something, it took an act of God to get her away from it. Under that pretty exterior and sweet smile was a charming bulldog . . . with a bite.

"Don't worry, we'll be careful. If we find the Cadillac, maybe we can reason with the guy."

Rose knew better. She also knew better than to argue or try and make Jill change direction. "Just mind yourself and be careful.

"As soon as we find out anything, I'll stop at the first payphone and dial you. OK?"

"I'll be waiting for your call." Rose agreed apprehensively.

With her index finger, Rose tapped the phone hook a single time, yet the receiver never left her hand. She was troubled, and the situation was getting serious. She had involved Jill in the search and now it seemed she couldn't get her out of it.

A bold move needed to be made and in a hurry. She wasn't about to sit in Gallup and wait for a phone call from Jill. Instead, she clicked the hook again and waited impatiently for the operator.

"I need SYCamore 7-2839 please." The operator connected the call with agonizing lethargy.

A polite voice with a Spanish accent answered, the whine of a motor being spun up filled the background.

"Del Toro Speed and Machine, this is Marty."

"Martinez darling," Rose put all the warmth into her voice she could muster, "how's the best hot rod builder in Los Angeles today?"

"Mrs. Rose! So good to hear from you, Senora! How is New Mexico?"

"New Mexico is wonderful, but we miss all of our friends out there." Rose's voice dropped suddenly, impatient and with an uncharacteristic urgency. "Martinez, I have a question. Have you ever heard of a man named Kreiger Koslov?"

The motor roared in the background, but her friend was silent at the other end of the line. She could hear him take a deep breath, contemplating his response, thrown off guard.

"Yes, I know who he is Rose," came the hesitant reply, "he's a very dangerous man. Why do you ask of him?"

Her hands went cold around the receiver. She couldn't remember such a somber reply from her old friend. "Martinez," she said with a shaken voice. "I need your help."

3:00 P.M., THE EL RANCHO HOTEL, GALLUP, NEW MEXICO

As Rose poured herself an early afternoon drink in an attempt to calm her nerves, she felt thankful for a friend like Marty.

Del Toro was anything but a novice when it came to handling the more unsavory element of Southern California's car culture. Del Toro Speed and Machine had long been one of Los Angeles's best speed shops and Marty knew everybody, the good and the bad. If anyone could help Jill from getting into trouble, it was going to be Marty.

The friendship between the two went back for over a decade. Marty, a war hero of the Battle of Leyte Island during World War II, was known around town as, "The Bull" and for good reason. His heroism was legendary. The story about how Del Toro charged the open battlefield at Kilay Ridge on a motorcycle, completely exposed and unarmed, single handedly saving three men's lives while taking fire that nearly tore his leg off had taken on near mythical status. The respected hot rod builder, who started his speed shop with the disability check he received from the military, was a constant, positive presence in the neighborhood, proudly representing VFW Post # 1053 every Veteran's Day.

It was in 1947, when Rose was working on *The Devil On Wheels*, that she found Marty. PRC Pictures needed her to find someone to take the contract for providing the custom cars for the film and the personnel to drive them. Rose connected with his shop through the special effects department at MGM as Del Toro had the reputation for building fantastic cars and cycles on time and under budget. Del Toro Speed and Machine was a perfect fit for Rose. It was to be the beginning of a lasting business relationship and close friendship between the two.

Over the next ten years Rose would call Marty to work on dozens of pictures, providing cars, motorcycles and personnel. The work allowed Marty to grow his business to a level of success he couldn't have achieved on his own. Rose Aspinall was a big part of that success.

3:00 P.M., DEL TORO SPEED AND MACHINE, PASADENA, CALIFORNIA

After Marty hung up the phone, he sat quietly, the industrial buffing machine and its compressor drowning out smaller noises in the busy speedshop. He abruptly stood, walked through the shop, and called his greasers to a meeting.

DANNY WHITE

3:05 P.M., KOSLOV'S CHOP SHOP, LOS ANGELES, CALIFORNIA

On the east side of town a different kind of conversation was taking place. In a rundown warehouse jammed full of cars being dismantled and stripped, an illegal chop shop operation was humming like a well oiled machine. Koslov looked over the 1957 Roman Red Lincoln Continental that was sitting on four, metal jacks. Its wheels, motor, transmission, interior and instruments, already removed. The gleaming metal body was all that remained. Boxes stacked nearby on wooden skids were addressed for Mexico awaiting the next shipping truck. Koslov strolled through the shop, inspecting the cargo.

It was nearly the end of the workday as the manager of Koslov's "business," Pacific Distributing, walked toward his boss, pointing to the next vehicle in line.

"Do you want us to start on this one? It's almost quitting time."

"No. Leave this one for me," the Russian whispered, running the back of his hand slowly along the car's stainless steel top. "I'll drive it over the weekend. A car like this should see the road one more time. We'll give it the treatment on Monday."

17

3:10 P.M., PASADENA, CALIFORNIA

The group walked out of Bob's Big Boy and into the warmth of the California sun. Before DJ started the engine, they were already planning their next move.

Annie and Jill were busy mapping out the routes to every spot that DJ squeezed out of the tire store clerk. Meanwhile, DJ, Michael, and Billy were having a serious conversation about what they might be up against. If they were to find Koslov, what were they going to do? There weren't any good solutions. To complicate matters, they were most likely being pursued by a Federal Agent as well.

"I understand that they need information about the accident," Michael deliberated with Billy, looking for some rational explanation, "but why come all the way to California to take the tapes?"

Billy pondered the question all day. Now, he thought he knew the answer.

"I'll tell you why," he straightened, enlightenment adding conviction to his words, "there are forces within the government that want to stop rock 'n' roll."

The statement drew confounded stares. Michael reasoned, trying to get a grip on Billy's theory.

"But the agent doesn't even know if you have the tapes. If Eddie told him everything about why you're out here, then he knows you're looking for the tapes too."

"More than that," Billy continued, way ahead of Michael and ignoring his comment for the moment. "Before these people stop rock and roll, they want to profit from it."

The pair sat silent, stymied by the outlandish concept. Now on the edge of their seats, they waited for what Billy might say next.

He urged them forward with his forceful, and convincing voice. "Think about it guys. What do you think those tapes are worth now since Buddy, Ritchie, and The Bopper have died?"

They absorbed the implications of Billy's words as he continued.

"Can you imagine what a record company could bank on those recordings over time? A label could release and re-release pieces and parts for decades." Billy slapped his hand on the dash. "These guys sold millions of records!"

DJ and Michael gazed blankly, realizing that it was possible.

Billy looked them squarely in the eyes. "It all comes down to this: what would a record label pay to keep those tapes from being confiscated or locked away?"

They looked stunned as the realization of the awful truth hit them. DJ finally mouthed in a low voice, awestruck at his friend's intelligence.

"Millions?"

Billy finished. "Millions . . . and then some."

Billy recalled reading an article in *The Clear Lake Mirror* the previous summer about the FCC's investigation into the Payola scandal within the broadcasting industry. The story outlined how the government wanted to stop the record labels from bribing broadcasting executives, hence, influencing them to play music from their artists. He reflected further within himself, staring out the window.

It's just the other way around. There are people in the government strong-arming recording labels via the threat of banning their artist's and recordings. It's perfectly logical that an official on the take would come after the tapes.

Billy's mind moved swiftly.

The Agent is looking for the tapes and using us as his bird dog at the same time . . . If we don't find the car none of this matters anyway.

"We've got the shortest route between all of the areas mapped." Annie sang out from the back seat, command clear in her voice. "I suggest we get moving. There's a lot of ground to cover."

Over the next five plus hours, the searchers covered every long mile of Foothill and Glen Oaks Boulevard, scouring each of the busy streets. More than once Jill thought she saw the same, black car behind them as they moved east to west across the valley.

8:00 P.M., THE VILLAGE INN,
GLENDALE, CALIFORNIA

The search on the streets of Pasadena garnered nothing. The evening was getting later and later, as DJ pulled into the parking lot of The Village Inn. The tiny, roadside restaurant was a local legend with car guys, and the last place on the list to look. Options were running thin.

The Village was a hangout for lake racers. The small, elite group of race car owners and drivers that set world land speed records on the dry lakebeds dotting the terrain around Los Angeles, were known for their fearlessness and devotion to the sport.

The Supercharged Fairlane rumbled loudly into the crowded parking lot as Little Richard's "*Long Tall Sally*" rang out from one of the cars in the crush. DJ walked into the congregation of more than a dozen race car owners and their rides, each of them a serious piece of machinery.

DJ was comfortable here. He felt as if any moment his Uncle Jim would step from behind one of the sleek power plants and clap him on the shoulder, excited to show him a new innovation in horse-power improvement. DJ fit in like one of the boys that just returned from a long vacation as the conversations flowed easily. He walked among the cars quietly introducing himself as he went. It was immediately apparent that Koslov and his bunch were not thought of kindly among The Village Inn faithful.

"Has he been here this evening?" DJ asked a small, spare racer as he leaned against his '34 Plymouth.

"Yeah, unfortunately," the man answered dryly. "They were out in force this evening."

"Would you have any idea where they might be going tonight?"

"Sure," the racer spat casually near the rear tire, wiping his lips with the back of his hand. "Anytime they show up in those kinds of numbers, they end up at Harvey's Broiler on Firestone Avenue in Downey. They'll be there tonight, looking for a race no doubt.

DJ remembered the clerk saying something about Downey but didn't ask him about it.

"Harvey's Broiler you say?" Double checking, keenly aware like Billy, that time was rapidly slipping away.

"You got it. Harvey's is the biggest carhop and cruising spot in the city. You can't miss it."

DJ thanked the racer, muttering under his breath as he walked back to the car.

We're closing in. If he's looking for a race, I'll give him one.

DJ slid into the driver's seat.

"Koslov and his gang left here about a half an hour ago. We need to get to a place called Harvey's Broiler on Firestone Avenue."

"Take a left going south at the next light," Jill advised, while Annie feverishly consulted the LA street guide.

Pulling back onto the street, DJ mashed the gas and sped off toward Harvey's. At the same time another car sped off as well, keeping plenty of distance.

After a long search, they finally picked up Koslov's trail . . . and company.

18

9:30 P.M., HARVEY'S BROILER, DOWNEY, CALIFORNIA

Are you serious?" Billy gasped, slack jawed to no one in particular as they approached Harvey's Broiler. Its "Fat Boy" sign glittered like a Casino on the Las Vegas strip while the Rockin' Roman's *"Downtown"* bopped and jived on XRKT.

"The mother ship has landed!" DJ exclaimed with a rush, leaning forward on the steering wheel, peering, round-eyed at the spectacle in front of them.

Growing up in the Midwest they had seen their fair share of restaurants and cruising locales. Harvey's Broiler, on the other hand, was a different story entirely. The place was like nothing they even knew existed. Cruising Harvey's Broiler was "Valhalla" for anybody with a car.

The gigantic sign that stood above the car-hop, beamed across the Southern California night: *"Harvey's Broiler-Restaurant-Coffee Shop-Drive In."*

"I'll bet you can see this place from outer space," Michael joked, craning his neck out the passenger window.

Waiting to get into the parking lot of Harvey's to "make the rounds," traffic was lined up for more than a city block, winding around the sweeping curve that led to the hottest cruising spot in Los Angeles.

"There must be a thousand cars here." Jill said, marveling at the spectacle.

As they turned into the main entrance, the grandeur of Harvey's came into full view. The glass and stone covered walls of the restaurant shot nearly 40 feet high. The colossal V-shaped canopies hovering over the carhop area were so brightly lit they looked like giant, incandescent kites flying against the darkened sky.

The Fairlane rolled by the front door, its reflection mirrored in the immaculate glass of the restaurant. The sheer number of hot rods, draggers, motorcycles, and customs that were streaming through, brought the "cruising," to "inching."

DJ threw an alert over the back seat, never taking his focus off of the bumper in front of him. "Eyes wide open everybody."

Every eyeball in the Fairlane scanned the jostling venue, vainly seeking a glimpse of the Cadillac or its thief. Cars were parked everywhere with trays of food attached to the doors. Car hops roller skated their way through the mass of vehicles, taking root beer ice cream floats, French fries, hamburgers, and thick slices of banana cream pie to customers milling around outside.

They were just about half way through the car-hop when a flash of emerald caught Michael's eye.

"There it is!" He shouted, pointing at the gleaming grill of the Cadillac, jutting out beside a black and white '57 Chevy. "Over there near the end of the row."

Billy almost shoved Michael into the passenger door as he shot forward to take a look, feeling an enormous sense of relief.

"That's it! That's Uncle Earl's Cadillac!" He could hardly believe it was the same car he left in the snow the previous Monday in Clear Lake.

DJ piloted the Fairlane carefully into a nearby stall while Michael glared furiously.

"Those guys in front of the Chevy were part of the bunch that jumped me at the Victory. The guy leaning against the Cadillac . . . that's–"

DJ didn't hear the rest, springing out of the car toward the tall, angular man in dark glasses with his foot propped against the bumper of the Cadillac. Slowing down, jamming his hands in his pockets, he sauntered closer. Billy and Michael marched tightly beside him.

"Nice car . . . Iowa plates! I just happen to be from Iowa myself . . . small world isn't it?"

Kreiger Koslov lifted his glasses and slowly took a drag from his cigarette, holding the smoke for several long seconds before exhaling it out like a dragon through his nose.

"Go away."

"Go away? You gotta be joking. I just got here." DJ's tight smile didn't reach his eyes. "Besides, you've got your greasy paws all over my car."

The response was immediate. Koslov's thugs, crouching in the Chevy slipped out with loud slamming doors and stood arm to arm with their boss.

The gauntlet had been thrown down.

"I've come three thousand miles looking for that car Koslov and I'm not going away." He could see the surprise in the lanky Russian's face when he called him out by name.

He took another drag from his lung rocket, ignoring DJ. He suddenly stood up from the Cadillac, his sallow nose turning towards Michael.

"I know you. Looks like you got beat with an ugly stick boy. You'll be getting the rest of what's coming to you Big Wheel."

"Bring it on, punk!" Michael's eyes sparked and his fists clenched, lunging forward at Koslov but not before Billy jumped between them. "I'm ready for you this time!"

"And I'm ready for you." Koslov said slowly, without flinching, cigarette smoke snaking around his head.

A crowd began to gather.

"Look Koslov, or Cosmonaut, or whatever they call you. Just hand over the car. It'll save you the embarrassment of losing it to me in a drag race."

Billy couldn't believe what DJ was saying. He kept the alarm from his face as his eyes tried to catch DJ's attention.

DANNY WHITE

We're supposed to be playing it safe, NOT challenging a criminal to a drag race!!

DJ stared straight ahead.

The Russian didn't respond, focusing beyond them, distracted by a movement in the throng of onlookers. The crush of gawkers began to swell. Among them, a group of men muscled their way through to the front of the crowd.

Their leader stopped, his compact, well muscled torso covered by a thin white t-shirt. Muted tattoos of long haired lovelies decorated his scarred, grease stained arms. His dark eyes, set in a lined face, grizzled with stubble, remained unmoving on Koslov.

The anger of being surprised again showed briefly in Koslov's face. Still, he mocked the man now standing beside DJ.

"Well, look who it is . . . the stunt doubles. There must be some "B" movie getting filmed around here tonight."

"Ah . . . you've got it all wrong, Gringo. We were just in the neighborhood and wondered what smelled so bad." Del Toro delivered the insult with a crocodile grin. "I should have guessed... *El Raton.*"

Billy shot a questioning glance at DJ with Koslov distracted by the unknown man, then looked over at him as if they actually knew each other.

"Good to see you again."

"Our friend Rose sends her best." Del Toro answered, with a short nod to Billy.

Koslov growled as he re-focused on DJ. "I have no trouble with you Del Toro. I'm just going to teach this loudmouth a lesson."

DJ returned Koslov's stony stare and continued to hammer at him. "I want the car. Let's have it."

The Russian's voice dropped to an evil croak. "You'll be walking on my dead body to make that happen, cornfield boy."

DJ ignored the insult, lifting an eyebrow, his reply cutting at Koslov.

"If you're not going to give it back, then be a man about it and let's race for it. You are a man, aren't you Cosmo?"

Billy knew they had gone too far. His insides writhed for Annie and Jill, daring not to chance a look back to see if they were well away from the coming rumble. There was going to be a race, or a fight. No way out.

"Back home we'd call it 'fish or cut bait time.'" Billy offered conversationally with DJ, his voice calm, ready for the fight.

"I like fishin." DJ grinned, still locked in the stare. "I'm not much on cuttin' bait. How about you Cosmo? Are you a runner or are you a stinkin' bait cutter?"

The dangerous Russian wanted nothing more than to jam the switchblade tucked in his boot into DJ's gut. He fumed inside and promised himself silently to get DJ, after the race, after he had the cars.

"All right, cornfield," Koslov ceded. "I'll race you for the Cadillac. If you win, it's yours. If you lose, I take your car and keep the Cadillac."

"He'll be racing my car."

Del Toro's statement took DJ aback, breaking his stare to glance questioningly at the solid presence next to him.

"This is none of your business." Koslov's barely checked venom whipped at Del Toro.

DJ tried to keep his thoughts together.

What's this guy doing? I can beat that Chevy with The King Bee. I know it!

Del Toro returned a mere half-glance at DJ before focusing again on Koslov. DJ knew the look and recognized it immediately. *This guy's old school!! Just like Uncle Jim! He's trying to tell me something!*

"Are you trying to get rid of me, Kreiger?" Del Toro crossed his arms, rolling up on the balls of his feet, feigning a surprised look as if having a new found inspiration.

"No! I know what it is now . . . you're just yellow."

Koslov clenched his teeth, scowling like a demon.

"It's easy to steal a car or cheat a man out of a drag race, eh Gringo? You only want the race you can win, not the race that takes talent."

Koslov raged inside, but revealed little emotion. The cracks were there nevertheless, and Del Toro recognized them. He was drawing the Russian in.

Cold fire flew out of Koslov's eyes like a pair of scalding ice picks.

"You'll get your race." Koslov finally accepted the challenge. "And your boy here better be ready. I call the place and time."

Del Toro turned slightly toward DJ with a question mark in his eyes.

Are you in?

"I could drive a milk truck and beat this chump." DJ promised heatedly, without hesitation.

"My car isn't a milk truck. I can assure you." Del Toro quipped and pointed through the crowd.

The mass parted as if Moses had commanded the Red Sea to make a path for him. Just then, Del Toro's beast of a machine materialized while the last few stragglers got out of the way. The 1931 Dodge Hemi Coupe crouched low on the pavement like a big orange and black cat ready for a jungle fight.

Koslov's malicious confidence faded. Many rumors existed about Del Toro's racer, but he had never seen it. The situation was not what he wanted but it didn't matter. The deal was done. If he won, he would come home with all three cars. It could be his best haul ever.

"Name it." DJ demanded, focusing only on his opponent.

Returning his slithering, snake-eyes to DJ, the Russian creeked. "The old Saugus Drag Strip in the Santa Clarita Valley. You better be there, or you'll never see this Cadillac again."

DJ couldn't help digging for the last word. "You're gonna wish I'd turned tail."

Koslov slid into the Cadillac, turned over its velvety smooth motor, and slammed the door. He lit another Camel, flicking the smoldering match at DJ.

"If you don't show, I'll track you down like a dog and beat that car out of you. You're not the only one with a surprise or two up his sleeve, farm hick."

As the Cadillac disappeared from the parking lot with Koslov's thugs in tow in the Chevy, DJ took a breath and thought about what had just happened. He asked himself as he walked toward the Dodge Coupe.

Who the heck is this guy Del Toro?

Just beyond the shadows of the parking lot security light, a tall, craggy faced man stood listening to the drama unfold. He flicked his smoldering cigarette to the curb, snuffed it out under a black Florsheim wing tip, and slowly began walking to his car.

The crowd scattered quickly, most of them already headed toward Santa Clarita. Billy was dazed. He thought about the new crisis, pacing around the Dodge, warily watching Del Toro and DJ approach the car. Jill and Annie stood near him, his hand possessively on Annie's head.

"We're glad you're here, but who the heck are you?" Billy asked the stranger directly.

"My name is Martinez Del Toro." He said with a kind smile, reaching out to shake hands with Billy and DJ. "Call me Marty."

"So you're a friend of Rose?" Billy said puzzled, instinctively turning toward Jill who shrugged in bewilderment.

"Yes," Marty took in their blank looks. "I've known Mrs. Rose for many years. She called on me to come and help you."

Annie was the first to recover, adding with no small amount of sarcasm. "From the looks of what just happened, it was a good thing she did."

"Mr. Del Toro," Jill asked. "Were you following us in a black four door car this afternoon by any chance?"

"No Miss, we've been in Zoo's Deuce all day."

"Zoo?" Billy asked, puzzled.

"Oh, excuse me." Del Toro held his hand toward his shop foreman, Kazuo Nakamura.

Kazuo "Zoo" Nakamura, Del Toro's ace speed shop metal-smith, sidekick, and war buddy, gave a wry salute toward his boss's new bewildered friends. He intoned directly.

"The car you're referring belongs to the federal agent that's been following you."

The news sent a shudder through the group.

"We discovered him tailing you in Pasadena a few hours ago. In fact, he's across the street waiting for us to leave."

DJ asked amazed and unnerved. "We've been followed all day by an agent and he's watching us speak right now?"

Marty nodded. "Rose told me about the tapes and the agent. It's easy to spot a guy like that in my neighborhood."

"Jeez." Billy breathed out a whoosh of recognition.

Marty motioned, turning to DJ. "We need to get going. Saugus is over thirty minutes from here. You can drive amigo. We'll talk about the race on the way."

DJ hoped Marty wouldn't guess his nervousness, but there was a race to win and knew nothing about the wheels he would be driving.

"You got it," he said, tossing the keys to the Fairlane at Billy then tucked inside the Dodge alongside Marty.

Marty turned to Zoo in a low whisper. "Fall in behind the Fairlane. I'm sure the agent will try and stay close."

As the three cars made a right turn onto Firestone Boulevard, Agent Stoneman fired up his black Studebaker Commander, popped on the headlights, and considered his next move.

10:30 P.M., FIRESTONE BOULEVARD, DOWNEY, CALIFORNIA

Marty watched the Studebaker intently in the side mirror of the Dodge Coupe, then turned to look through the radically chopped rear window at Zoo's flashing headlights, the signal they agreed on. The blow had been delivered.

Keeping one eye on the road and the other focused on his rear view mirror, Zoo watched a thick cloud of ink-like smoke billow from the tailpipe of the Studebaker, enveloping the car. Slowing to a stop near the corner of Firestone Avenue and Old River School Road, the car's headlights stuttered twice then dimmed.

Zoo chuckled. "Finally, the half-pound bag of confectionary sugar left over from our Dia De Los Muertos party has come to some good use!"

10:45 P.M., OLD RIVER SCHOOL RD, DOWNEY, CALIFORNIA

Stoneman spent fifteen minutes under the hood of the Studebaker looking for something obvious, hoping for a loose battery cable or a simple fix. He found nothing. The gunked up engine refused to turn over, prompting him to kick one of the Commander's heavy, white-walled rear tires in frustration. His patience forfeited long ago, he was burning precious time that he couldn't afford to lose.

Sitting in front of a chicken coop on the curb, a nauseating aroma from the poultry farm was blowing in his direction, mixing with the odd, sweet smell coming from the Studebaker's tailpipe.

Somebody made me! He shouted suddenly, the breeze fanning his anger into a rage.

He savagely slammed the door on the lifeless car, then paced and stomped up and down the asphalt. The lights of Harvey's Broiler gleamed in the distance. A pay phone was just across the street.

Palming his black wool Pork Pie hat, he tore off in a dead run for the restaurant, promising to make them pay for every step he took.

DJ concentrated intently on Marty's directions as the newly formed drag racing partnership headed north to Santa Clarita. He adjusted to the massive difference in horsepower, the layout of the pedals, shift position and stance of the Dodge with relative ease, remembering the lessons of his Uncle Jim.

The interior of Del Toro's car was as much a 1940's era fighter aircraft as it was a hot rod. With its Corsair shifter grip, Stewart-Warner aviation gauges, and pinup girls painted on salvaged war-bird aluminum, the cockpit of the Dodge was like being launched back in time.

"So tell me what you knew back there that I didn't?"

Marty put his hands together and cracked his knuckles. "The first thing is: you won't be racing that Chevy."

"What do you mean I won't be racing the Chevy?"

"Koslov races a gutted out '57 Chrysler 300 that he stole from a banker's kid in Beverly Hills, not the Black Widow."

"That's a heavy car." DJ stated, matter-of-factly, "I'll cream that thing with this baby."

"Wrong." Marty retorted. "That machine of Koslov's has more aluminum in it than steel. Those guys are surgeons with a cutting torch if you haven't heard already."

DJ remained silent, digesting the new information. "What about his motor?"

"It's a 392 Hemi with a blower and two-fours." Marty said shortly, a warning in his tone.

"What?" DJ gasped, as if someone just punched him in the mouth. "You're kidding me, right?"

Marty paused. "I don't joke about this stuff. There's one last detail . . . he doesn't run gasoline."

DJ's arms began to tremble slightly. "Now wait just a dog-gone minute here. I didn't know anythi–"

"He burns nitromethane crammed full of all sorts of other nasty concoctions. You wouldn't have had a chance in the Fairlane." Marty said, without heat.

"But nitro's been outlawed by the National Hot Rod Association for almost two years in drag racing, right?"

"Sure it has . . . at sanctioned races." Marty agreed, and added, "I think you will concur with me that this is no NHRA sanctioned event. It couldn't be further from one and Koslov could care less anyway."

DJ was taken aback for a moment, realizing the enormous mistake that Del Toro saved him from back at Harvey's. He didn't consider the fact that the Russian might bring a different car to the race.

"I should have figured on the dirty tricks. Now I'm really glad I kept my mouth shut when you showed up."

"Don't feel bad." Marty admired DJ's audacity. "You couldn't have seen it coming. He counts on surprise to win races. There's a reason he's undefeated after all."

"How does he get away with it?"

"Most of the people he races don't realize what the deal is until they show up to race. By then it's too late."

DJ interjected, realizing the scheme. "So if they try to back out, he cuts his gang loose, beats the daylights out of them, and takes their car anyway."

Marty nodded his head. "You got it amigo. It's safer to go ahead with the race, which most have no chance of winning."

DJ knew he was going to be in for the race of his life, and was eager to learn about the Dodge. It was his only chance to walk away a winner.

He eyed the controls. "So, what's the lowdown on this machine?"

Marty grinned. "You can be tough with her as long as you handle her with authority. If she knows you're in control, she'll run like a banshee for you." He paused. "If you don't, she'll kill you."

DJ shook his head, in an effort to dispel the fear that tightened in his chest.

"Don't worry muchacho, you're up to the task." Marty assured him. "I wouldn't have put her on the line in this race if I didn't think so. Besides, she's undefeated too . . . sixteen straight."

"Why *did* you put your car on the line for us?" DJ wondered, even more aware of the debt he owed Del Toro. "You don't even know us."

Marty tried to shore up his confidence. "Rose told me all about you guys and what you were doing out here. I'd do about anything for her. Besides, I gave your car the once over when you and Koslov were having it out . . . I could tell you were a runner."

The conversation suddenly stopped. Link Wray's *Rumble*, oozed from the coupe's radio, barely audible over the steady roar of the giant motor.

Marty gazed aimlessly out the window as they passed the entrance to the Mission Hills Cemetery bordering Sepulveda Boulevard. Two lanterns glowed faintly at the entrance. Marty spoke quietly, lost in a moment of sadness.

"They buried Ritchie Valens there this morning. No one should die at seventeen. That kid meant an awful lot to us Latinos. We loved the music he made."

DJ was frozen with Marty's words, suddenly remembering the incident with the careening station wagon on the way back from Mason City.

We were only a mile from the airport and there wasn't anyone else on the road. They crashed at about 1 a.m., it had to be them! Our paths are crossing again!

DJ sat, transfixed by the coincidences.

"DJ?" Marty felt the young man behind the wheel of his car go still. "What is it?"

"Uh, nothing." DJ shook off the feeling. "We were talking about the car—

"Like I was saying before, she's got a history and her own personality."

"Let's hear it," DJ said, anxious to know anything that might help him.

"I got her a few years ago in a ghost town called Lookout, north of San Francisco. Zoo and I drove up to take a look at it, and found it covered in tumbleweeds in front of an abandoned mine shaft."

"Tore up bad?" DJ asked.

"Yeah . . . just a rusty shell, but Zoo is a magician with metalwork. The body is his creation, the motor and everything else is mine." Marty remembered.

"I was told it once belonged to a man named Jack Gunn, a saloon owner in Lookout back in the early 1930s. Legend has it that he used her to run illegal liquor during Prohibition." He laughed, stroking the dashboard like a favorite pet, "she's definitely got a mind of her own!"

"Well let's hope that my mindreading techniques are as good as my driving skills tonight," DJ joked feebly, "how about the mechanics?"

"She's brutally powerful." Marty answered bluntly. "Under the hood she's got a Fuel Injected 354 Hemi out of a '56 Chrysler New Yorker. But it's not exactly stock," he said with a wry smile. "One other thing . . ."

DJ's mind spun like a flywheel, trying to take it all in.

"Why do I get the impression you're gonna drop another bomb on me?"

"We'll have to change the fuel pump, bolt on a different intake and change a few other things for the alcohol set up."

"Alcohol?"

Marty grinned. "Yeah, we're setting the motor up for alcohol tonight. It won't take us long to switch it over. Zoo has all the stuff in his car. Got any questions?"

DJ laughed. "Sure. Where's the ejection seat lever in this thing?"

11:10 P.M., SAUGUS DRAG STRIP, WHITE'S CANYON ROAD
SANTA CLARITA VALLEY, CALIFORNIA

The night was black as pitch. The eerie darkness disturbed only by the flickering lights of cars snaking their way down the canyon to watch the match race.

The dust filled air around the abandoned airfield was perfectly still as DJ pulled the Dodge to a stop, hitting the kill switch on a quarter-mile section of the runway known as the Saugus Drag Strip.

Word of the impending pink slip race spread like a California wildfire, and the onyx colored night brightened. Thrill seekers from across the city began arriving, positioning their cars along the asphalt, resembling a long string of battery driven landing strip lights.

Annie, Michael, Billy, and Jill took up spots at the end of the strip near a tall oak tree, the drag strip's official finish line. On the other side of the giant tree sat the Cadillac. Nearby, one of Koslov's lackeys kept an eye on the dusty beauty, but he wasn't the only one with the car in his sights. Billy and Michael were honed in on the car like hawk's stalking their prey, and weren't about to take their eyes off of the race trophy for a second.

At the top of the strip, DJ and Marty were surrounded by the employees of Del Toro's shop. The preparations were well under way on the motor as DJ worked on the fuel pump and Del Toro worked on the Fuel Injection for the Hemi. Together they went about the task of fitting the big coupe with the alcohol modified equipment, tweaking the car for the race.

"He's got a bag chocked full of tricks does he?" DJ asked, butterflies danced in his stomach as he scraped the remnants of the old fuel pump gasket off of the block.

"You've got the car to win with, don't worry about the tricks," Marty warned. "It's going to come down to who's the better driver kid."

With the weight of the night sitting like an anvil on his shoulders, he found it hard not to think about what was riding on the race. Catching himself drifting, he re-focused expertly on bolting the fuel pump back into position with the same precision that Marty and Zoo were applying to the fuel delivery system.

"I'm ready farm hick, let's get it on." The Russian yelled, firing up his Chrysler.

The creature shot flames three feet out of its open headers, protruding from two rectangular holes cut in the front quarter panels of the 300. The ground quaked under the big car's tires, its power plant shaking it with an evil rumble. The hellish sound was accompanied by the smell of nitric acid and propane, the elements of the highly volatile nitromethane fuel . . . and something else.

DJ had been around nitro before with his Uncle Jim but couldn't make out the odd smell. Something more sinister in nature was swirling in the air. One thing was for certain; the black and gold Chrysler was cackling with rage, seemingly angry at being turned into a Frankenstein-like race car. Its interior, once a beautiful black calf-skin leather, was replaced in the front by a lone bucket seat. An aluminum fuel cell was strapped into the rear compartment where the back seat should have been. Both were sorry substitutions for the original, luxurious upholstery.

He glanced over at Marty, looking for an answer.

Marty yelled at DJ over the howl of the Chrysler as he made the final carburetor linkage adjustments

"It's hydrazine. The Russian's use it in their space launch and missile programs. That's the other reason they call him the Cosmonaut. He's playing a dangerous game with that stuff."

Behind the wheel of the Allis-Chalmers tractor orange coupe, DJ cranked the hemi over. The alcohol guzzling elephant winced and shook the car like a rag doll in a pit bull's mouth, cracking to life with a thunderclap. He laughed out loud, realizing the car that once ran illegal booze for thirsty silver miners was now drinking the stuff herself. *She should be right at home.* He thought.

What misgivings he might have had about his chances of winning the race, faded as he put the car into first gear and headed for the starting line.

The concussion of sound from the Dodge hit Koslov's ears like a lightning strike, not expecting Del Toro's car to run alcohol. With the stench of it now floating through the air, there could be no doubt.

Tonight I'm pulling out all the stops. Koslov promised himself, maneuvering his car beside DJ at the line.

★★★★★★★★★★★★★★★★★★★★★★★★★★

FEBRUARY 8, 1959
A DRAG RACE AND THE SPACEMAN

★★★★★★★★★★★★★★★★★★★★★★★★★★

20

12:00 A.M., THE RACE, SAUGUS DRAG STRIP, SANTA CLARITA, CALIFORNIA

The opponents idled slowly toward the starting line as both cars quaked with restrained power. A sense of challenge charged the night as the cars sat side by side, much like a pair of chariots would have done in the Coliseum of Rome two thousand years earlier. There would be only one winner. No second chances.

Marty stuck his head inside the coupe's window. "How ya doing kid?"

"I'm ready Marty. The track looks just like Great Bend back in Kansas."

"Good." Marty stopped. "Hey amigo."

"Yeah?"

"You're going to be a legend 1320 feet from this line," he smiled a wily grin, "now get after it and take this chump down."

A girl that was at the parking lot at Harvey's earlier emerged from the crowd, clutching a checkered flag to her breast, stopping between the cars.

The adversaries began inching to the line, braking, inching closer to the line, and braking again. The flag bearer halted the pair on the starting mark for what seemed an eternity as the two racers stared stoically down the track, unflinching and cold. Just then, she lifted the flag high above her head, and in a split second slammed it to the ground.

The reek of burning rubber and fuel mixtures immediately assaulted the air. Both flew across the starting line, neither car's front tires touching the pavement, roaring through the cloud of caustic smoke that enveloped them. Emerging from the smoldering haze, the racers seemed to have been transformed into tormented and ghoul-like characters, great beasts leaping from the bowels of the netherworld looking for revenge.

DJ shifted into second gear, his tachometer nearing 6,800 rpm.

Dangerous . . . watch it. He warned himself.

The raw power of the coupe screamed as it sucked the alcohol through its injectors, fueling the massive pistons. He was running the race his way, piloting the Dodge arrow straight down the strip . . . but Koslov was a bumper in front of him and pulling hard.

Patience. He fought the urge to put the pedal on the floor, but did not. Sweat began to slick down his hair and trickle between his back and the seat.

Let third gear pull as far as it'll go. I'll give it hell in fourth.

The cars screamed, door panel to door panel down the asphalt.

Koslov's car roared, flames flying from its headers, licking at the coupes' front wheel, singeing its orange paint.

Wait. Wait. Wait. DJ refused his impulse to shift, his hand steady on the pistol grip as the coupe's carburetors begged for more alcohol.

"NOW!"

He slammed the transmission into fourth gear, mashing the pedal to the floor. The effect of the big gear was immediate, hurling the Dodge down the strip with a mighty leap. Pulling its front wheels from the ground and erasing Koslov's lead. In a split second he drew a full car length on the Russian faster than his opponent knew what hit him. The hunter had now become the hunted.

Panic consumed the man they called the Cosmonaut as the two cars closed within 300 feet of the giant oak tree, growing taller in the distance as they drew closer.

Koslov was in trouble, running out of time, and losing. The tach inside his machine teetered on 7,000 rpm, burning like the rockets of the Cold War the hydrazine was designed to launch into space. The 392 howled as he crushed the accelerator against the firewall.

The motor was pleading for mercy. With its gears wound out, and way over the red line, Koslov edged the mighty Mopar to the passenger side door of the Dodge but it was too late. The 392 was melting under the assault of the hydrazine with nothing left to give in the contest.

The daunting motor belched one small puff of white smoke that exited both front fender wells then detonated into a garish fireball. The howitzer-like blast sent a collective and horrified gasp through the crowd of nearly two hundred, causing the throng to scatter as shards of metal flew through the air.

The blower from the 392 came crashing through the windshield while the transmission heaved itself through the floorboard at Koslov like a mortar round. Shuddering under the immediate reduction in speed, the Chrysler jerked violently to the left, narrowly missing the Dodge.

DJ glanced at his rear view mirror, burning with the reflection of the firestorm that enveloped Koslov and his car as he crossed the finish line in an orange flash. Annie, standing in front of the oak tree, kept her eye on the stopwatch. The game was over.

As DJ slowed and turned, he saw Marty running as fast as he was able to down the strip. Behind him, a wall of flashing police lights was bearing down hard.

This is just what we need . . . Gumball Machines. DJ swore, breathing heavily.

In the lead cruiser, Karl Stoneman was perched angrily in the front seat. DJ gritted his teeth, swung the car around, and circled back to get Marty.

"Let's get out of here now!" Billy yelled, as Annie and Jill jumped into the Fairlane while Michael took off on a dead run towards the Cadillac. Tackling Koslov's thug at the knees, both hit the ground at full speed. Michael's ribs ached painfully from the fall, but kept his grip on the struggling guard.

"Not this time," Michael growled, pounding the thief's face into the sandy dirt. He grinned lopsidedly, jumping over the hoodlum whom he left pummeled and face down. Throwing himself into the Cadillac, he sped toward Billy and DJ, already near the rear exit.

From the window of the coupe, Marty yelled at Billy as DJ sped through the giant plume of dust left by the rush of cars trying to escape the airfield. "Long Beach Pier . . . 30 minutes."

Stoneman watched in disbelief, stuck in the massive traffic jam of cars. Through the billowing smoke from Koslov's mortally wounded racer, he saw the tail lights of the orange coupe and the Cadillac disappear past a four-by-eight sheet of plywood with "EXIT" spray painted on it in big, red letters.

Tangled in the melee of cars scattering wildly in every direction, Stoneman could only fire a string of obscenities in their direction. There would be no catching them tonight.

21

12:35 A.M., LONG BEACH PIER, LONG BEACH, CALIFORNIA

At the waters edge, Billy leapt out of the Fairlane as DJ came running from Del Toro's Coupe.

"Was that a wild ride or what?" DJ whooped with a big Iowa holler, throwing his arms around Billy.

"You did it DJ!" Billy shouted, amazed at the raw display of driving prowess. "You did it!"

"I think this trophy belongs to you guys." Michael grinned, yelling from the Cadillac as he put the car into park and joined in on congratulating DJ.

Billy gave him a slap on the back. "Thanks, Michael. It would've gotten away again if it wasn't for you."

Looking at the Caddy, he realized; *I have it back! The Emerald Lady has returned!*

He hesitantly walked to the trunk of the car with a death grip on the keys that he kept safely in his pocket since they left Iowa, knowing the lock wouldn't be frozen this time. Fumbling nervously...the trunk popped open.

He reached behind the spare tire much like a child would reach under a pillow, hoping to find some small treasure, or maybe a couple of quarters left by the tooth fairy. Then, his hand touched the leather strap on the case. It was waiting for him, just as it was left in the frigid cold in front of his Uncle's house.

"Amigo," Marty asked. "Is it there?" The others stood silently behind him.

"Yes it is." Billy smiled. "All of it!" The collective breath they were all holding let loose as they crowded around the recorder. In the midst of the celebration, DJ asked reluctantly.

"Not to rain on the parade here, but does anybody know if there's even any music on those tapes?"

The jubilant noisemaking suddenly stilled.

"Oh come on, don't make me feel like a blockhead." DJ defended his inquiry. "It's an honest question."

"No, you're right. It's time to take a listen." His friend agreed with excitement and apprehension. "All the levels looked good when I recorded it, but it was my first recording, anything could have happened."

The recorder sat on the trunk lid of the car. Billy's friends huddled close around him in a show of support, an anxious look of suspense on their faces.

Billy set the small reels in place on the recorder, clamping them down and carefully threading the tape under the lifters. Gently, he pulled the tape across the capstan and between the pinch rollers, attaching its crumpled end to the take up reel.

Nervously he rubbed his forehead and looked over at Jill. Her smiled calmed him. Then, he reached up and pressed the small, gray "Play" button.

Click.

The reels jerked. A miniature light bulb in the VU meter quivered, and a faint, amber glow eaked from its lens. Then, as if someone pulled its plug, it slowly dimmed. He tried it again. *Click.*

This time there was no movement in the small machine whatsoever.

"Dead batteries!" He groaned to sky above. "What is it with me and dead batteries?"

DJ wise-cracked. "Show's over folks! No refunds, no returns. Get your jackets at the coat check. We hope you've enjoyed yourselves! Goodnight!!"

Michael began to cackle, his eyes squinting in a big smile. Then Jill and Annie joined in. Finally, Marty and Billy let go in a fit of laughter too.

Billy howled. "Guess that says volumes about any career I thought I may have as a recording engineer!"

"Billy, I've got a proposition for you," Marty said, his side still hurting from the laughter.

"Right now I think we need one!"

"There's a reason I asked that we meet here." Marty gathered himself.

"When Rose and I spoke earlier about the agent, she feared he was trying to take these tapes from you maliciously. I agreed with her. We all know what's going on with rock 'n' roll these days and how the government wants to control what's on the radio."

Over the prior few days, Billy thought of what to do with the tapes if he got them back. His determination that they be put to some positive purpose ignited once again.

Marty continued with caution. "They'll find you sooner or later Billy. Most likely that agent will show up in Clear Lake looking for you. When he does, you'll have no choice but to give him these tapes. Rose suggested that if we were lucky enough to recover the recordings, we should take them to Sam Sanders at XRKT and ask him to broadcast the music on his station as a tribute to the musicians."

Jill interrupted, incredulous. "Are you talking about Sam *The Spaceman* Sanders?"

DJ's eyebrows reached skyward. "The disc jockey from the radio station we've been listening to this weekend?"

"That's exactly who I'm talking about." Marty answered, proudly.

"But . . . he's a phantom." Jill held out her hands in an expression of ignorance. "No one's ever seen him."

"Well, young lady." Marty answered, the smile broadening on his brown face. "I can tell you he's not a phantom! In fact he's a friend of mine. He's a friend of Rose's too!"

Marty hurried on with his suggestion, plainly reading the mistrust on Billy's face.

"I'm not talking about giving him the tapes to keep. He's already offered to broadcast the tapes . . . tonight."

"Tonight?" Billy said, more bewildered.

"Think of it this way," Marty posed, "if the agent gets the tapes, and he will, who knows what will become of them? It's possible the music may never be heard again."

Marty paused, waiting for Billy to consider his advice.

He thought about the show at The Surf. It seemed so very long ago already. The uplifting energy of Buddy's voice was intoxicating as the thrumming of Waylon's Fender bass resonated through the floor and Tommy's melodic guitar lines vibrated in response. The utter synchronization of a thousand souls merged into a joyous celebration of music. With Marty's proposal, he saw a way to spread that magical moment once more.

"That guy must have a million listeners. Can we really do that?" Billy's eyes rounded at the enormous opportunity Marty offered.

Marty shook his head with a grin. "Yes my friend we can. Besides, it would mean a lot to Ritchie's fans here in Los Angeles. This was his home town after all."

Billy turned to his friends.

There was no need to ask. In unison they all surged forward, eager to honor the lives cut tragically short. After all of the trials they overcame to get the tapes, the answer was hardly in doubt.

Billy turned to Marty, his eyes shining with the prospect. "Let's do it!"

"Andale', andale'," Marty whooped with a flourish, leading everyone to the dock. "The Spaceman awaits!"

"So you know where he is?" Annie asked, after listening intently to the interchange.

"Yes I do, sweetheart." Marty pointed toward the dim lights of Catalina Island twinkling in the distance. "He's right out there."

"He's not on an island, he's on a ship." Michael interjected, as Annie began to question Marty on the aspects of the island. "I read about it in *The Times* on Friday."

They continued further down the dock, the moonlight shining with soft brightness on the sheltered waters.

"The article said he broadcasts illegally from a ship off the coast somewhere in Mexican waters right?"

"Illegal?" Billy shook his head and laughed. "That's just wonderful!"

"That's right Michael." Marty nodded approvingly. "But it shouldn't be illegal. He's just exercising his First Amendment Rights. Its part of what we fight for as Americans. When the government starts telling us what we can and can't listen to, it's trouble. They're trying to do that with rock 'n' roll."

"Mexico is a long way from here." DJ interjected, "how are we—

Marty grinned. "Mexico is indeed a long way from here, but the Spaceman isn't in Mexico."

They stopped at the waters edge and piled into a mighty speedboat, shifting gently with the moving tide. The motors howled as the cool pacific water twisted and gurgled underneath the duel propellers. Marty threw the keys to the Dodge at Zoo then slammed the throttle to the wall, speeding toward the western waters of Catalina Island.

1:35 A.M., THE PACIFIC OCEAN OFF THE COAST OF CALIFORNIA

Most people thought Sam Sanders broadcast his show from some isolated lagoon off the coast of Mexico or in the Sea of Cortez, just as the newspaper stated, far away from the prying eyes of the U.S. government. It was precisely Sander's plan and just the way he wanted it. Everyone believed he was in Mexico when it fact, only the XRKT transmitter was on the other side of the border.

The Spaceman's border blaster pumped out a mind numbing 60,000 watts of power, far exceeding stations licensed to do business in the

United States. To have that kind of output, the transmitter needed to be in Mexico, a country with few regulations regarding radio stations.

"The High Octane Pilot of The Radio Rocket Ship," as Sam liked to refer to his position at the station, came and went on the radio dial at 1550AM. It was part of the strategy. Never making a commitment to a routine, made it nearly impossible for the authorities to find him.

One night he might be on at 9:00 p.m., the next at midnight. His shows were usually long, high energy affairs, lasting until he wore himself out or pulled or muscle. The Spaceman was so popular that the Rocket Ship faithful in Spaceland would sometimes wait hours for him to begin broadcasting.

A Sam Sanders show was a cross between a vaudeville act and a southern evangelical sermon on Sunday morning. He always delivered an exciting and entertaining show, featuring a wide cross section of rock 'n' roll artists of the day. As an independent station he could play whatever he wanted and artists flocked to his congregation, knowing that Sam possessed a very special and direct connection to the listening public.

This relationship with the artists allowed Sam to get his hands on music months before it was released on mainstream stations in the United States and the kids ate it up. To say you heard it first meant something. And, on any given night, if you listened to the Spaceman, you just might get those bragging rights.

His operation confounded his competitors on the American side leading to no small amount of jealousy. In turn, the contention created all sorts of rumors about the man.

There were countless theories floating around about who was behind

XRKT. Some said it was an extension of XERF in Del Rio, Texas. Others figured he was funded by the higher ups at Atlantic Records in New York. Scores of people ventured that Sanders wasn't Sanders at all. Rather, he was a well known radio personality from the east coast, frustrated that he couldn't get away with doing the show he wanted to do on his regular station. It all added to the mystery and confusion. No one really knew any answers, again, it was just as The Spaceman wanted it.

The ocean was calm as the twin Corvette V-8s of the Crystaliner speedboat hummed across the breakers. The small ripples of their wake made the sea look like a finely woven Persian carpet, laid out perfectly in the biggest living room in the world.

Taking time to reflect for a moment as the surf thundered past, and the smell of Jill's perfume lingered in the breeze, Billy relaxed. Even on the small transistor radio inside the boat, tuned to XRKT, The Penguins, *Earth Angel*, sounded angelic.

Billy took in the ocean's majesty, quite different than the calm of Clear Lake. Beyond the magnificence of the ocean, the real beauty of the night radiated from Jill. He held her hand gently as they sat beside each other in the speedboat while the salty spray from the ocean waves occasionally floated through the air.

Annie's voice broke the sweet, momentary silence of the group on board, diverting DJ's stare from the water, drawing his attention back into the boat.

"Guess what your time was tonight DJ?"

"Gosh, I haven't thought about it. It was good enough to win and that's what counts."

"It was 9.98." The little timekeeper stated, a touch deflated by his lack of enthusiasm.

"I don't believe you!" DJ straightened, and crunched his eyebrows, mouth agape. "That can't be. You've made a mistake!"

Annie quickly informed him that she had made no mistake, now happier with his reaction.

"It was probably quicker than that but I took off a few tenths for my reaction lag to the flag drop." Annie huffed a bit at his doubt in her timing abilities. "I'll stand by my 9.98."

"Are you sure?"

"Nooo dowwwtt," she responded slowly, as if she were talking to a child.

DJ rose to his feet and proceeded to give a proud proclamation.

"Hear ye hear ye." He cleared his throat. "I've been informed by our distinguished time keeper, Miss Annie Daniels—"

He turned with a chuckle, whispering in Billy's direction as the waves continued to fly by.

"Billy, give me a drum roll . . . Gene Krupa style."

Rat a tat tat. Rat a tat tat . . . rang out as Billy pretended the rail of the boat was a snare drum; his hands the legendary drummer's sticks.

Grandstanding like a Carnival Barker, he announced in a stately voice.

"I, Darrell James Evans did set a new world record tonight for a stock bodied car in a one-quarter-mile contest. Feast your eyes on the unofficial King of the 1320!"

Applause erupted from the boat and Marty hollered something in Spanish that no one understood.

Billy stood clapping his hands in the festive moment. "You're the world champion right here right now, DJ. I don't care what any book or official has to say about it."

As the congratulations continued, the lights of Avalon materialized off the boat's starboard bow, appearing as an ocean bound cluster of fireflies, hovering in the distance. The Crystaliner began to sing a lower tune as the speedboat slowed, leaving a wide, zipper like pattern on the ocean's surface. Anticipation was high in the boat.

"It's definitely not a rocket ship." Billy observed with a chuckle. "It looks more like a Cutter."

The markings were obvious on the 150 foot decommissioned Navy vessel. Its flag snapped in the breeze and Billy sized it up.

"A red flag with a white stripe . . . a diving boat. It's a beauty, innocent looking white. No guns. A play toy of the rich and famous . . . not a Pirate radio station." Billy concluded his assessment of Sam's radio station, *"a perfect disguise."*

22

2:10 A.M., XRKT RADIO, THE COASTAL WATERS WEST OF CATALINA ISLAND, CALIFORNIA

Two mammoth-like guards came to the rail of the ship as Michael threw a mooring rope in the direction of its ladder.

"Hola!" Marty called out to the security duo.

"Cómo está?" They answered, obviously having met Marty before.

As they walked through the doors of the enclosed stern, outfitted with black windows that even the strongest of sunlight would have a hard time penetrating, an unexpected artistic melting pot boiled in front of them.

"We're not in Iowa anymore Tin Man." Billy muttered in DJ's direction on their way in.

"Ya think?" DJ whispered back.

The amazing festival-like atmosphere of the rogue radio station was astonishing. Cultures collided before their eyes in a scene that was part Hollywood Golden Era, part 19th century speakeasy, and one hundred percent rock 'n' roll.

Wading through the cigarette smoke hanging in the air like a London Fog, wafting its way around a chandelier attached to the 10-foot ceiling, they stopped to take in some of the entertainment.

Singers were hashing out harmonies. Musicians were trading saxophones riffs while a group belted out tight doo-wop harmonies. Beyond them, a young man in black leather played a Latin tango rhythm on guitar for a woman in a mint blue dress that sounded like Etta James.

Music was alive, and everywhere on Sam's ship.

"Where else in the world is this happening?" Billy asked Marty, enthralled in the scope of what was going on around them. "So many people from so many different backgrounds coming together to make music?"

"Nowhere else as far as I know," Marty replied, "but it could be happening everywhere. The world would certainly be a better place. I guess it's all about how we look at life and the spirit of how we want to live it my friend."

Billy craned his head, trying to take in as much of it as he could. "This is what music was meant to be."

While they stood, entranced in the atmosphere, a gentleman dressed in a perfectly tailored gray flannel suit with a blue silk tie, slowly made his way to them through the bustling crowd. He appeared more as a parent chaperone at a high school prom than anyone who might be among such revelers on board the ship.

"Mr. Sam asked me to bring you to the studio," the man said. "Follow me please."

Walking to the command center, in the middle of the ship, they stopped. In the middle of the wall, a large sheet of glass was surrounded by tiny Christmas lights. Behind the glass, a man with sweat pouring down his face was doing the duck walk and twirling a Shure Model Fifty-Five microphone by its cable.

Their escort opened the door leading into the bustling studio, and held his hand out before them. "Ladies and Gentleman . . . I give you The Spaceman."

The explosive black disc jockey was decked out in a floor-length black-and-white polka dotted coat, over a crimson red velvet shirt sporting a white fur collar. His purple suede boots with matching teardrop fedora hat, flashed in the lights of the control room as he performed a show he knew his audience couldn't see. It didn't matter. They could see him through their radios.

The visitors watched, awestruck as Sanders delivered his rock and roll sermon . . .

"Whooooooaa, we gonna come and give it to ya tonight, uh! I want everybahhhdy that can hear the word uh huh. I said I want evvvverybody that can heeeearuh the word. Stop watcha drivin'. Stand up! Dance on the hood and say; I love Rock and Roll!! That's what The Spaceman tellin' ya uh huh. Now come on and get up on the Space Ship wit me. Here he come, the night is young! Turn it up lowwwd! 'Please, Please, Please' . . . James Brown!!!"

The Godfather of Soul blasted out of the studio monitors as Sam put the microphone back on its stand, taking a moment to wipe the sweat from his forehead. He walked over to his humidor, lit a Cuban cigar, and turned to Billy.

"The Spaceman welcomes you to his space ship." Sanders said, shaking Billy's hand.

"Thank you, Mr. Sanders. Uh, I mean Mr. Spaceman. This is my little sister Annie, and my friends DJ, Jill, and Michael."

He eyed the recorder and the tapes.

"Mrs. Rose called today and said you might be coming." The smoke from the cigar wafted through the room. "You recorded these at the Winter Dance Party show in Iowa last Monday right?"

"Yes sir."

"The Spaceman was hoping you all would make it out here tonight. Rose told him all about the trouble."

"I'm glad too," Billy chuckled uneasily, "but there's just one thing."

"What's that?" Sanders looked puzzled.

"We haven't played them yet. My recorder's got dead batteries."

Sam motioned to his assistant. "The Spaceman got a closet full of batteries friend. Let's load that thang up and see if they got any music that wanna come out!"

Sanders sat the Nagra on top of his broadcast desk, loading the recorder with batteries. The little amber light on the VU meter came to life, glowing brightly this time. Sanders connected the output of the recorder to the patch bay of the studio and keyed the microphone.

"It 'tis 2:51 but the party's just begun at X-R-K-T. The Intergalactic Rock 'N' Roll Spaceship is blastin' through the Spaceland with 60,000 watts of love!! Listen to me now. The Spaceman wanna bring it down a minute. Then we gonna bring it back up. Right now let me tell ya, we got somethin' special tonight to send out to everybahdy. I wanna take a minute. I said I wanna take just one minute to recognize some fine musicians we lost this week in a plane crash way out there in Iowa. You know who I'm talkin' 'bout; The Big Bopper, Mr. Ritchie Valens, and Mr. Buddy Holly."

Sanders whispered into the microphone like he was saying a prayer while a musician took a seat behind the Hammond organ that was sitting in the corner. She began to wobble chords behind the Disc Jockey reverently.

"They gave us some great music while they were with us in this earthly Spaceland. Now, they in that great universe in the sky where we all wanna go some day . . . a long, long time from now . . . but tonight!"

Sanders jumped up and started pacing the floor, one hand on the microphone and the other hand high in the air, waving back and forth. His finger pointed to the heavens and the organ player picked up the tempo.

"Tonight my friends we got some very special guests. They come all the way from Iowa to visit The Spaceman heruh tonight. Been through a lotta' hard times . . . I said a whole lotta' hard times, an troubles, an tribulations trying to get what we gonna share with all you lovely people."

Sam strutted through the studio, working the room like each of his listeners was right there in the studio with him.

"Fo' ev'rybahhhdy out there. I said for ev'ry bahhdy that didn't get to hear this show. My friend Billy and his pals done brought it to the Spaceship fo' ya' tonight. An' you gonna hear it on X.R.K.T. babies!"

Sanders jumped high in the air, landing squarely on a chair sitting by the desk.

"Listen up close y'all. The Winter Dance Party's coming to ya!"

"Can I get an AMEN for Rock and Roll music tonight uh huh?"

"I said can I getta AMEN tonight?"

The crowd inside the radio station began to scream, caught up in the moment with Sam.

"It's The Bopper, it's Ritchie, and Buddy Hawwwwley!!

Click...

The tape rolled . . . and the crowd cheered.

Dion Dimucci shouted over the deafening roar.

"It's been a great show tonight right?"

Applause and screams echoed through the Surf Ballroom, ringing off of its curved roof.

"How about a big round of applause for The Big Bopper, and Mr. La Bamba himself . . . Ritchie Valens! And the band; Waylon Jennings,

Tommy Allsup, and this fabulous drummer, who's pulled double duty all night, hard at work playing drums for Ritchie and me. You know him from his appearances on *The Ed Sullivan Show*. You know his top ten hits: *That'll Be the Day, Peggy Sue, Oh Boy*, and the list goes on and on."

The crowd came unglued, causing the tape to distort as "the drummer" took off his cowboy hat and traded it for his signature, black horn-rimmed glasses. He grabbed his guitar, then jumped toward the microphone.

"Get ready for the last rock and roll show of the evening. Here he is! "Let's hear it for the drummer . . . I mean uh . . . The incomparable Buddy Holly!!!!!"

Buddy hit the chords to *Gotta Travel On* and the music sprang from the studio monitors. *The Winter Dance Party* lived again.

A party broke loose in the packed studio the likes of which they had never seen as Sam played every tape, non-stop. *Rave on, Chantilly Lace*, and *Donna. Oh Boy, That'll Be the Day, Wishing, Come On Let's Go*, and *Not Fade Away*. The hits kept comin' as the tapes kept rolling.

Billy listened with satisfaction, realizing that he and his friends were helping the musicians give the fans one last gift. It was more like a joyous wake than a radio show. Jill gazed up and kissed Billy as the raucous celebration roared.

She asked him softly, pitched for his ears only.

"Was it worth it, Billy?"

He looked softly back into her eyes, tilting her chin up with a gentle finger, kissing her tenderly. "Of course it was worth it. I met you didn't I?"

Annie, spying on them from nearby, was not impressed. "Ewww . . . gross!"

Twirling around a set of twin sisters that were part of the revelry on board, DJ and Michael danced like it was New Year's Eve.

"Oh no . . . twins!" Billy laughed, his arm around Jill, finally at peace with himself and the world.

DJ whooped. "What a night Billy! What a night!"

Sam was caught up in the music, doing the peppermint twist and the mashed potato at the same time. As he whirled around, twisting to the music, his eye spun past a converted closet that the station used as an equipment room, catching a glimpse of the power supply rack. He stopped dancing, immediately alarmed. Something was wrong. The light was off on the broadcast voltmeter and its needle was lying motionless on the dead pin. He ran over and put his hand on the supply . . . cold. It had been off for quite a while.

3:25 A.M., THE COAST OF CATALINA ISLAND, CALIFORNIA

The radio was tuned to 1550AM in the coast patrol boat of the Los Angeles Police Department. There was no music. Crackling meekly, only the sound of white noise and an occasional click or pop could be heard coming from the small speaker in the console of the boat.

Reaching down and rotating the volume knob all the way to the right, Agent Stoneman turned it up.

"It's a beautiful sound." He crooned tunelessly to himself as the boat sped toward Catalina Island. Suddenly, in a mocking tone he imitated the last words he heard before the station went dead; "The incomparable, Buddy Hol—

The introduction was interrupted and cut short a half an hour earlier thanks to the handy work of his operatives.

"How do they know Sam Sanders?" The agent asked himself, baffled yet thrilled with the stroke of good luck.

3:28 A.M., CERRO VELADERO MOUNTAIN, BAJA OF CALIFORNIA, MEXICO

The echo of shotgun blasts silenced long ago, absorbed into the rough terrain and valleys surrounding Cerro Veladero Mountain, near Tijuana, Mexico.

The single, two-inch padlock, once latched on the rusty metal door of XRKT's transmitter lay on the ground. A contorted mass of twisted metal fragments.

Thieves swarmed around the radio tower's large equipment room, quickly loading radio gear into the back of a rickety flatbed truck. They were given their orders weeks earlier. The deal was clear: Kill the transmitter. Take the equipment as payment. Leave nothing behind.

The bandits put the old truck in gear, laden with equipment that once powered XRKT and slowly began the narrow descent down the mountain's dusty gravel road.

The mountaintop returned to darkness as the taillights disappeared. The bright red light atop the XRKT transmitter flickered briefly, its residual power bleeding away.

Ritchie's hit single "La Bamba" blasted through the speakers as he and The Big Bopper, joined Buddy on stage at the Surf for an encore, singing the song like there was no tomorrow.

"Lights, Boss!" The security guard rushed into the control room, raising his voice over the din. "Lot's of them, about five miles out."

Sam immediately knew what it meant. He turned the music off and spoke urgently.

"Listen to me, friends! We need to get to the speedboats right away. There's no need to panic . . . but *the man* is on the way."

Sam led everyone calmly outside, trying to minimize the coming melee. The control room emptied quickly and everyone collectively rushed for the door.

Sanders and the security guards grabbed what they could and began helping people toward the stern of the ship, into the small boats that would take them to the shore.

THE LAST ROCK AND ROLL SHOW

On deck it was a scramble. Musicians came running with their guitars and saxophones. The drummer took only his snare drum, leaving the rest of the kit where it sat. The upright player wasn't far behind, dragging the giant violin shaped bass in his wake.

Sam focused on loading his guests into the speedboats as the lights of the shore patrol became bigger and brighter on the horizon. Both of Sander's boats were jam packed, already headed toward the lights of Los Angeles at full throttle.

Billy eyed the Crystaliner they came in on, about half full and still moored to the ship, rocking back and forth in the sea. There was little time. Making sure that Annie and Jill got to the boat, crowded out any other thought in his mind.

"Jump on, Annie!" He yelled at his little sister, who took a leap onto his back, wrapping her arms around his neck. Turning, Billy reached for Jill's hand. "Follow me sweetheart, we're getting off of this thing!"

DJ and Michael were right behind, with the twin sisters in tow, leading them to the Crystaliner, clutching two sets of high heels.

"There's no one driving the boat, Billy!" DJ gasped, helping the girls down the ladder that led to the Crystaliner.

"I've got it, boys," Marty reassured them, nimbly stepping around people to get to the cockpit of the boat, cranking over the big motors.

"We're heavy, Billy!" Marty yelled as the boat rumbled, sitting low in the water beside the big ship. "We can't take anymore!"

"We've got one more!" Billy shouted.

"I don't know if we can do it Billy!"

Sam yelled at Billy. "The Spaceman is staying behind. Get outta here! I'll stay on the ship."

"NO YOU WON'T!" Billy roared, grabbing the disc jockey by the collar of his polka dotted jacket, sending him flying into the boat. "Rock 'n' roll needs you too much!"

Billy untied the mooring rope and barked at Marty. "GO!!!!"

Marty pegged the throttle, throwing everyone backwards as the ocean speedster leapt forward. The sea gurgled and churned behind the boat, throwing saltwater into Billy's face as he stared back at the abandoned ship. Suddenly, he realized that something was left behind, a very important something . . .

"THE TAPES!!!!"

He yelled toward the ship, a knot forming in his stomach, gripping the seat and watching helplessly as the big ship became smaller and smaller with the increasing distance.

He could only watch as the police boats slowed then moored against the ship. Officers scampered up the ladders, covering the deck.

Stoneman stood on the XRKT ship, watching the speed boat lights disappear around the northern edge of Catalina.

"Do you want us to go after them?" The Los Angeles county police sergeant asked.

"No . . . we have the ship." Stoneman said, walking to the control room. "This pirate radio station has walked the plank and died. We'll just let them sing the blues."

Looking around at the station he tried to locate and shut down for almost a year, he gloated in his conquest.

"They can start measuring the drapes for my corner office in Washington."

Among the mess left in the hasty retreat were stacks upon stacks of records along with piles of equipment and gear.

"Start packing it up," Stoneman barked at the Police detachment, not interested in wasting any time. "I want it out of here tonight."

Taking a seat in the chair of his nemesis, he relished the victory. Then, he noticed the small recorder, still warm to the touch with a stack of tapes beside it.

"What do we have here?" He murmured curiously, picking it up to get a good look at the white identification tag attached to the top of the recorder.

"Property of: Billy Daniels Clear Lake, Iowa." He said aloud, snickering.

He leaned back in Sam's desk chair and chuckled hoarsely.

"This is gonna save me a trip back to that deep freeze in Iowa," he laughed again, handing the recorder and tapes to the police sergeant, "put this with the rest of the stuff."

Stoneman's victory was complete. No more lame assignments. No more freezing in cheap motel rooms. Soon he would push Marlowe out of the way, and take over where the old man left off.

DANNY WHITE

5:00 A.M., LONG BEACH PIER,
LONG BEACH, CALIFORNIA

The ousted partygoers scattered in every direction after disembarking on the pier, fearing the police could show up at any second. With no lights headed their way, the gang rallied up.

Zoo and a few of Del Toro's employees were waiting with the cars.

"What happened?" Zoo asked. "We've been listening in the car but the radio was dead. All we heard was the introduction . . . then static."

"You're joking, right?" Marty asked, his voice rising in his disbelief.

"No." Zoo's shoulders sagged, scrubbing his face with his scar-crossed hands. "We wondered what was going on when we saw the police lights on the water."

Billy leaned against the Cadillac with a dejected look on his face.

"Did you not play it?" Zoo asked.

"Yeah we played it." Billy mumbled. "We thought we were playing it for everyone. It sounds like we were only playing it for ourselves. I'm sorry."

Billy felt a crushing weight descend on him. He knew the music was lost with no chance of a recovery this time. The realization of what had happened deflated everyone. Jill comforted Annie who was quietly sobbing, the experience finally becoming too much for her. Everyone else just stood in a daze, staring at the ground.

THE LAST ROCK AND ROLL SHOW

DJ sat on the Fairlane, a look of confusion and sheer exhaustion drew deep lines on his face. "I hate losing."

The joyous celebration from just an hour earlier, turned into silence. Just then, a familiar, energetic voice came from behind.

"Why the long faces, babies?" The voice of Sam Sanders perked.

"No one got to hear the show Sam." Billy said sadly.

Sam spun around. "No one got to hear the show! The Spaceman didn't just hear you say that did he?"

"It got cut off before it started Sam."

"The Spaceman's ears musta been lyin' then, 'cause he heard it! Yeah, he heard the whole dang thing!"

Sam began pacing, tailcoats fluttering as he spun around the other direction, hands waving, looking up to the brightening sky.

"The Spaceman musta been dancing by himself, to music that whadn't even playin. His eyes musta been lying when he saw everybahhddy dancing at the radio station."

Sam stopped, and pointed his finger at each one of them in turn. "He saw you and you and you dancing on the chairs. You heard it didn't ya?"

They looked at each other and nodded.

"You didn't fail!" Sam stomped his velvet boot on the ground. "You succeeded and you don't even know it! Everybahhhdy that was heeere tonight gonna carry what they heard in their hearts for a long, long time. They gonna pass it on and it'll live forever! That whudn't no rock 'n' roll show!! It was a REVIVAL!! That music got reborn again tonight. It was lost and you found it! That . . . my brotha and sista is something to be thankful for."

He stopped for a moment, looked out into the ocean, then smiled with a little laugh.

"The Spaceman lost his boat tonight *and* his radio station!"

He amended himself wryly.

"Actually the boat was a rental but anyway who's keepin' track? You see . . . tonight at the station, well, that was a very special moment. It couldn't last forever! You all gave, and were given a great gift . . . that couldn't last forever either. None of the good stuff lasts long anyway."

Billy's frown turned into an understanding grin. There was a murmur of agreement among the gang with the realization that Sam was right.

"The Spaceman gotsa go kids." He said as his car arrived. The gray-suited man, impeccable, now with a driver's cap razor straight on his head, opened a door silently for him.

"Keep your ears open, you just might hear The Spaceman on the radio again one day! WHOOW, I feel good!! And remember; rock 'n' roll ain't neva gonna die!!!"

Sam slid into the back of his baby blue Lincoln Continental, waving goodbye with his purple velvet fedora flapping wildly out of the window.

24

11:00 A.M., THE LOVELLE RESIDENCE, BEL AIR, CALIFORNIA

The sun perched warmly on the horizon, drifting in the California sky above the vast Pacific Ocean as Billy sat in a lounge chair on the veranda with a cup of coffee. Birds chirped brightly in the breeze as Ricky Nelson's *Lonesome Town* played on the radio, but it wasn't XRKT.

He began to think about life and what it might bring. It was time to get on with it. There was college to deal with and a career to chase. His boyhood was behind him.

Getting the Cadillac back to Iowa before his Uncle returned wasn't going to happen. Trying to get it back home and then pretend that nothing ever happened seemed like a stupid and dishonest idea now. It would not have been the right thing to do. It was time to face the music, explain what happened, and take his medicine.

There were phone calls to make. Annie was going to miss school on Monday and probably Tuesday as well. His parents would be worried, probably angry, and would certainly expect an explanation . . . they deserved one.

Then of course there would be Uncle Earl to answer to. It all seemed trivial. Everyone was safe, that's what mattered most.

The recordings were gone but the little tapes had taught him some valuable lessons over the last five days:

Great moments are fleeting.

Consequences are real.

Life and the joy we give to others is precious.

Above all of these thoughts, there was Jill. Who would have thought a few days could have affected him the way they did? She was a dream come true and the thought of leaving her to go back to Iowa was heavy on his heart. He didn't want to lose her, but didn't know for sure if she felt the same way.

He walked back into the kitchen where Michael, DJ, and Annie were having a bite to eat. Jill of course, made a great lunch and packed some food to take with them on the long trip back.

"You ready to hit the dusty trail pal?" DJ stood next to him, his hands engulfing a piece of toast and a donut.

"Yeah." Billy looked around. "We better get going. Clear Lake is calling."

Michael was going back with them. He needed to clear things up with his Dad, make his apologies, and try to make amends for what he did. There would be time for California later.

"Billy," Jill's voice came from the veranda.

He walked out to her in the warm sunshine.

"You know the summers in California are quite nice," she said shyly, looking towards the ocean, "maybe you would like it here in the summer?"

Billy watched her profile, her hair flying in light strands of honeyed gold around her face. "Is that a weather report or . . ." He leaned down and kissed her, caressing the soft skin at the nape of her neck.

"No, Billy." She smiled. "That's an invitation."

TWO WEEKS LATER AT A GOVERNMENT WAREHOUSE ON THE OUTSKIRTS OF RICHMOND, VIRGINIA . . .

Come on back with it." The warehouse manager motioned, stepping backwards, his hand in the air, waving the forklift driver forward. "To the right a little, whoaa, that's good. How many of these do we have?"

"We've got three of 'em." The forklift operator said, flipping through the shipping documents labeled: *Evidence: Radio Equipment and Supplies Case #2859100569.* "It says here that Agent Karl Stoneman will call for this stuff in a couple of weeks."

"Stoneman?" The manager looked up from his review of the boxes, looking as if he wanted the forklift driver to recheck the documents. "Karl Stoneman? Over at the OBS?"

The forklift operator's eye traveled down the manifest authorization page.

"Yeah, that's it. Stoneman; the Office of Broadcast Security."

The manager hitched up his pants.

"That guy's not going to be calling anytime soon. I heard from upstairs that he got busted . . . caught up in a Payola scam. Said he took money from all kinds of people with his boss Marlowe . . . those guys have always got their hands in the kitty somehow."

"So what do you want me to do with this stuff?"

The manager pointed to the back of the twenty acre facility.

"Just take it all back to Building 89 . . . Long Term. I've got a feeling it's going to be here a while."

25

PRESENT DAY 3:00 P.M., HERSHEY, PENNSYLVANIA

Snow was everywhere, piled high and deep, covering the town like a layer of white chocolate over chopped nuts. It was a bright day, and much to the delight of the residents of Hershey, the weather started to warm a little, unlocking diamond-bright droplets, steadily dripping from the icicles that hung from every rooftop.

Snow meant there was money to be made for young Benjamin Kolbe and his three buddies, the town experts in the art of shoveling snow. The four friends could do a wax job on most driveways and connecting sidewalks in less than 20 minutes. It turned out to be a banner day.

At three o' clock in the afternoon, after shoveling the white fluff for nearly eight hours, the gang of four had cleared twenty five driveways; a great day for shoveling snow and a better day for their wallets. Tired and soaked with sweat, the eleven year olds made their way back home, each fantasizing about where they were going to spend the money they earned.

One wanted to buy vintage comic books off of the internet. Another wanted a new football and another a down payment on a bike. Ben was just happy to have some money in his pocket so he wouldn't need to ask his mom and dad to borrow any. There was a recession on and times were tough. Every penny counted.

The friends took turns at dragging the wagon home, loaded with snow shovels, a broom, and an empty Igloo cooler. While taking his turn at pulling the homemade snow wagon, Ben eyed an elderly woman attempting a descent of her front steps. The woman, with hair as white as the snow on the ground, appeared frail and cold. Her coat was torn, frayed and at least a couple sizes too big for her.

As they came closer, Ben stopped the wagon and loped easily up the front walk, grasping her hand as she began to stumble.

"This is no weather to be out in, young lady," he quipped, helping her down the precarious ice encrusted steps, her arm tucked underneath his own.

"Oh, thank you," she said, almost inaudibly, "just trying to get out to the mailbox."

Ben looked down the frozen, snow covered sidewalk leading to the mailbox, doubtful that she could make the trip safely.

The snow was heavier on her property. Shrubs were completely covered and the very top of a "FOR SALE" was sign barely visible in her front yard. In the driveway, a huge snowdrift covered a seemingly abandoned car up to its door handles.

"How about me and my friends shovel your sidewalk and take care of that driveway so you can get your car in the garage?" He asked with a smile on his face.

"It's nice of you to offer young man but I can't afford it," she said with a shake in her voice, "and besides, the garage is full of junk that needs to be thrown out. It's been sitting there since my husband passed away almost six months ago now."

Ben turned and looked over the old woman's head at his buddies still on the street. They were tired and cold, but with a look from Ben, they cast in line behind their leader one by one, picking up their shovels and setting to work. Their pockets were full of cash, now it was time to do one for free.

"There won't be any charge ma'am," he said, helping her back into the warm confines of her house.

She thanked them with trembling hands, surprised at their kindness. The boys went at it like a chain gang, shoveling the sidewalk leading to the mailbox, scraping the dangerous ice away beneath it. They tackled the snowdrifts encasing the car then brushed the early model Mercury Marquis off with the snow broom. The snowy car wash made it sparkle in the sun.

Forty five minutes later, the driveway was spotless, the sidewalks were clean, and eight large boxes were stacked at the end of the driveway ready for the garbage truck to haul away. Ben knocked on the door.

"We're all done," he said proudly, "you can go out there and dance on the driveway if you feel like it!" The old woman could see the sweat pouring off of the boy's faces. She thanked them, apologizing again for not having the means to pay them.

As the boys walked down the steps, she offered.

"If there's anything in those boxes that you might want, just take it with you. My husband bought the stuff at a government auction a few years ago. I was told there wasn't anything there worth much."

The smile on her face was worth more than anything to the boys. They said their goodbyes, and walked back out to the sidewalk.

"Anybody want any of this junk?" Ben asked the others as he began peering into each of the boxes. The only pile that looked promising contained a bunch of wiring, an old radio and a bunch of other electronic looking pieces.

"Nah," one of his buddies shrugged, dropping a microphone clip back into one of the opened boxes.

"I'm going to take this bunch here for the heck of it . . . might be able to make somethin' out of this stuff." Ben heaved the box on the wagon, grabbed the handle, and began the slow trek back home.

The fireplace in the living room of the Kolbe house was a sight for sore eyes. Warmed by the fire and a hot chocolate, Ben began going through the junk.

"Watcha got, son?" His mother called out from the kitchen, her sudsy arms immersed in a sink full of dishes.

"Just a bunch of junk an old lady gave me for shovelin' her driveway." He replied, dragging the pieces out and laying them on the floor.

His mother pointed a concerned eye toward the grimy electronics, now scattered across the floor. "Hey, watch the carpet, young man! That stuff looks dirty."

"OK. OK." He said, spreading some newspapers out on the floor, continuing to drag the contents from the soggy cardboard.

The box was deeper than he thought and contained more junk than expected. He emptied it just as the newspapers protecting his mother's carpet spilled over with stuff from the mess of electronics.

Holding up a hand full of reels, plucked from the bottom of the box, he hollered toward the kitchen.

"Hey, mom . . . "

"What?" She stuck her head around the corner, drying her hands on a dishrag.

"What are these?"

She adjusted her glasses, focusing in on the objects.

"Those are analog tapes son," she chuckled, "that's how great grandma and grandpa used to listen to music before compact discs and mp3s were invented."

"Really?" He asked bewildered. "There's music on these things?"

"There could be," she said walking back to the kitchen, "but they don't make machines to play those with anymore."

He studied the weird looking reels with brown tape wound around them.

Kinda looks like that packing tape we get from the UPS man. "Hey Mom!" He hollered again, throwing his voice in the direction of the kitchen sink.

"What?" She rolled her eyes, now exasperated. "I'm trying to get some work done here. You need to get that mess out of the living room and *into* a trash can."

He studied the small faded white labels stuck to the plastic reels.

Property of Billy Daniels-Clear Lake, Iowa

He walked toward the kitchen and craned his head around the door toward his mother. Amazed and puzzled that music might somehow live on the dusty relics from the past, he asked his mother innocently, as only a child can do.

"Mom . . . who's Buddy Holly?"

EPILOGUE

Billy came back to Clear Lake but it was only to say goodbye. He spit shined the Cadillac and returned it to his Uncle, who was surprisingly, unconcerned about it. Earl told Billy he was just happy they returned safely. Besides, he already had his eye on the new '59 Biarritz Convertible. He proudly proclaimed that no one at the club was going to have a car with bigger tailfins!!

Billy had no intention of letting Jill Lovelle get away and thought that just maybe she might want to get caught. He returned to California in the summer of 1959 and the two enrolled together at San Diego State University. Billy earned a degree in engineering and started a company, manufacturing audio and video surveillance products. Jill went on to get a PhD in Marine Science and landed a job at Sea World. The two married in August of 1962 and had two children. Billy and Jill Daniels still live in San Diego and enjoy spending time with their three grandchildren any time they get a chance.

Sadly, the Lovelle home in Bel Air was burned to the ground in November of 1961 by the Bel Air-Brentwood wildfires. The Lovelle's didn't rebuild and decided that maybe it was time to retire and enjoy the rest of life. With no intention of closing the company, they knew the perfect person to turn operations over to.

Rose Aspinall became a full partner in the business, returning to Los Angeles in early 1962 with her mother, shortly after her father passed away.

DJ graduated from Clear Lake High School in 1959, joined the Special Forces of the US Army, and was stationed at Ft. Knox, Kentucky. He became part of the elite "Hell on Wheels" tank command unit at Ft. Knox and later moved into the intelligence field in Washington D.C. He continued working for the military throughout the Vietnam War as well as with other intelligence agencies. He married his wife Marie in 1967.

In 1978, after his son Colt was born, he and Marie moved back to Iowa. DJ took a position in the State of Iowa Department of Internal Affairs where he still enjoys his senior intelligence status and refuses to retire. He still owns the '56 Fairlane.

OBS Director Marlowe and Agent Stoneman got a free place to live for a couple of years . . . in prison.

Michael Minton returned home to Clear Lake and mended the relationship with his father. As he walked up the driveway of Earl Willingham's home on his way to make an apology, he picked up a shaggy dog scampering across the yard, assuming it belonged to the Willingham's. When Earl answered the door, with Michael holding the little dog that had evaded him for such a long time, the two became instant friends.

They named the dog "Jet" and took him to the Clear Lake retirement home where he was gainfully employed, keeping the old folks company.

Michael went to work for Earl cleaning boats without pay in the summer of 1959 to make up for what he did. When summer was over, Michael went back to Los Angeles. Before he left town, Willingham asked him to stop by the golf club on his way. He handed the young actor an envelope, "Break a Leg" was written on the outside . . . inside there was a $1,000 in cash. The two kept in touch via an occasional letter, and an annual Christmas card, until Earl passed away in 1987.

Under his stage name Michael went on to act in numerous films during the '60's, '70's and 1980's. He never returned to Clear Lake and is now retired in West Hills, California, doing an infomercial or two every now and again.

Annie received a scholarship to Purdue University in West Lafayette, Indiana after graduating from Clear Lake High School. Upon completing her undergraduate studies, she traveled to California to be near her brother and to complete her doctorate at the California Institute of Technology in Pasadena. She has enjoyed a long and illustrious career working at the Jet Propulsion Laboratory, near the Cal Tech campus.

Koslov's theft ring was broken up that night at the Saugus drag strip. The police arrested many of his Pacific Distributing employees while they were trying to flee the scene. As part of a plea deal, those arrested informed the authorities in regard to the whereabouts of the chop shop and shortly after, it was dismantled.

Krieger Koslov was morbidly disfigured by the explosion at Saugus and suffered multiple internal injuries. After eight months in the hospital, a day before he was to be released, a nurse found his room abandoned. He was never heard from again.

Marty Del Toro continued his work as a master craftsman of custom cars and motorcycles for many years. He prospered in his partnership with the film industry, and so did the community he lived in. Marty's efforts and good will helped thousands of youth around his neighborhood to go on to great success in life.

Widowed now, Marty still lives in Pasadena, the town that he has always loved and has always loved him back. Fifteen grandchildren make sure he is never alone and Marty is always willing to share a story or two about the early days of hot rodding if you ask him.

One of those stories concerns the disappearance of the '31 Dodge Coupe.

In the summer of 1963 Marty began to experiment with the use of hydraulics, hoping to create an alternative drive system for automobiles. The following summer he built an innovative rear engine lake car using a hydraulic motor that employed direct drive mechanics. The results were jaw dropping.

He took the car to the El Mirage dry lake outside of Victorville, California, with Zoo to make a few runs. What they accomplished was no less than revolutionary. On one sunny day in July, the new fangled hydraulic lake racer turned in a speed of over 150 miles per hour.

Patents were applied for the technology, but the excitement over their work was short lived. Shortly after receiving a letter from the U.S. Patent Office informing them that their patent applications were being declined, the speed shop was broken in to and robbed. The lake car and the '31 coupe were taken.

The lock was never broken on the door, and the shop was left perfectly intact with the exception of the missing cars, and a file cabinet full of technical data. Marty has long suspected the cars were taken by greedy, oil industry barons that have stolen or suppressed such technology for decades.

To this day, the mighty coupe and the lake car that vanished without a trace have never resurfaced.

Sam Sanders became the blue print for an entire generation of Disc Jockey's that followed him. The spirit of "The Spaceman" still lives in the hearts of everyone that loves Rock 'n' Roll.

ABOUT THIS BOOK

I wanted to take a moment to delineate some fact from fiction. Buddy Holly, Richie Valens, J.P. Richardson, and Roger Peterson, the pilot of a Beech Bonanza aircraft, died in a plane crash on February 3, 1959, following a show at the Surf Ballroom in Clear Lake, Iowa. As fate would have it, Tommy Allsup was not on the plane that night, having lost a coin toss for a seat on the ill-fated flight in which there were no survivors. To this day, Tommy is alive and well, living in Oklahoma, and still performs for fans around the world.

All of the places on Route 66 existed in February of 1959 or still exist. Griffith Park, Harvey's Broiler (now Bob's Big Boy Broiler), the Victory Drive In, Bettery's, and the Roosevelt Hotel are just a few of the places that are still in existence today. Sadly, other notable sites along Route 66 and southern California have been absorbed into history, existing only as the odd picture, postcard, or memory from the past. The vehicle makes, models, motors and speed equipment in the book are accurate and period correct for 1959. The OBS characters are products of my imagination and completely fictitious.

From 1957 through 1960, the FCC proved to be one of the more convoluted, and troubled segments of the federal government. For example, the Director of the FCC was forced to resign his position in 1960 by Dwight D. Eisenhower, the President of The United States of America. The reason? At the time, the FCC Director admitted to having accepted favors directly from the broadcasting industry. I will leave the details of this seemingly under-handed set of events for you to ponder regarding the government's crusade against rock-n-roll in the 1950's. Look it up, it's interesting!

The Last Rock and Roll Show is a product of my childhood in small town Indiana, the proud son of a rock 'n' roll singer who experienced the 1950s music generation first hand. My Dad furthered my musical passion as he shared his plentiful, personal rock-n-roll stories from the 1950's with me. My early induction into the joy that music brings, along with my own personal experiences as both a studio and inter-national touring musician, further cemented the central character music plays in my life.

Previously, there was an actual search for a lost recording. However, the quest wasn't for Buddy Holly's final performance, rather; for an elusive Elvis Presley performance. Back in 2005, Robert Reynolds (of Grammy award winning Mavericks' fame) contacted me to transfer some 1950's analog tapes (over 200 in total) to Pro Tools digital files. I transferred the tapes at our family owned recording facility, 16 Ton Studios, located on Music Row in Nashville, Tennessee.

Based on my upbringing, and fascination of music from the '50's, I find any analog recording from this decade particularly appealing. Upon hearing the tapes, I quickly realized they were not some generic tape collection, replete with familiar material. These tapes were the personal recordings of renowned Country Music Hall of Fame Member, Mr. Hank Snow, "The Singing Ranger." The tape collection had been tucked away in Hank's home in Madison, Tennessee for close to 50 years. I was immediately captivated at the prospect of hearing rare recordings from an era which shaped my soul.

Whatever was on those tapes contained material devoid of a label and music which had not been heard in decades, since Hank's machine ceased to work many years earlier. As I began working with the tapes, my goal was to keep the transfers as authentic as possible when converting them from the analog to the digital domain. In order to accomplish this, I purchased Hank's broken Mono 1955 Ampex 350 tape machine, fixed it, and went to work.

Although, much work was to be done, I had hoped to discover the phantom recording of Elvis Presley's 1954 performance at the Grand Ole Opry. Rumors of this tape's existence circulated for decades and I hoped to find this pearl somewhere within the mountain of dusty tapes.

For those unfamiliar with Hank Snow's background, he was Elvis' co-manager in 1954-55 and operated a company called *Jamboree Productions*. The other half of the management team was headed up by Cornelius van Kuijk, more commonly known as Colonel Tom Parker. Parker eventually broke away from Jamboree Productions and went on to manage Elvis until *The King of Rock and Roll's* untimely death in 1977.

During the 1950s, Hank Snow was a frequent performer on the Grand Ole Opry, and was known to record many of his Opry performances. Hank was performing at the Opry on October 2, 1954 and personally introduced Presley. This was to be the only time Elvis would ever grace the Grand Ole Opry stage.

As the tape rolled by, I discovered countless lost performances by scores of country music's finest performers of the 1950's. Hearing these rare live treasures transported me back to the very first time I listened to music-the music I was raised on and grew to love. There were recordings of Porter Wagoner, Marty Robbins, Jim Reeves, and Ernest Tubb just to name a few. Jewels would come out of nowhere including one of my favorites; Hank Williams doing a commercial for BC Headache Powders. Unfortunately, the Elvis recording was conspicuously absent.

I know it's out there somewhere . . . fast forward.

In the summers of 2007 and 2008, I had the great honor and good fortune to play bass on tour with Tommy Allsup. Tommy was Buddy Holly's guitarist on *The Winter Dance Party* Tour in 1959 and survivor of the famous "coin toss" that saved his life . . . and led to the end of Ritchie's.

Both tours were performed in the United Kingdom along with Kevin Montgomery, the son of Buddy's best friend Bob Montgomery, from Lubbock High School in Texas.

During the summer of 2008, I created the story line of this book while traveling with Tommy and Kevin in a camper van as we performed across England and Scotland.

Both of our tours received a warm and enthusiastic reception from the fans of the United Kingdom, who are some of the best in the world in my opinion. As music devotees ourselves, we were deeply touched and moved by the enthusiasm and fervor from the audience.

During the tour, we received many intriguing questions. These questions were the catalyst of the book you hold in your hands.

Most enthusiasts of music from this era were well aware of *The*

Apartment Tapes, which were Buddy's famous acoustic demos recorded at his New York City flat that included *Peggy Sue Got Married* and others.

However, these famous tapes left more questions than they answered. Specifically, were there any bootlegs?

Did anyone record Buddy Holly and his band on that fateful night at The Surf Ballroom, or possibly at one of the other venues on The Winter Dance Party Tour in 1959? Despite continued industry networking and searching, the honest answer is that no one really knows for sure and the question still remains unanswered to this day.

However, I believe that one day, on some errant Internet site, or ubiquitous online advertisement, garage sale, or even a nondescript newspaper ad may appear, containing a seemingly innocuous description such as:

```
FOR SALE: One shoebox full of old tapes
without     labels,     purchased     by     my
Grandfather  at  a  yard  sale  decades  ago.
Have  no  machine  to  play  them.  Artist
unknown. $10 or best offer.
```

The music of Buddy Holly, Ritchie Valens, and J.P. "The Big Bopper" Richardson still defines the very heart, soul, and essence of what Rock 'n' Roll is all about: pure, fun.

Their music will never die . . . or Fade Away.